Joshua Wiggins and the King's Kids

Stories for family devotions

CHARLES BEAMER

BETHANY HOUSE PUBLISHERS
Minneapolis, Minnesota 55438

Dedication

To: Shannon, Chris, Jodi, Joshua
and all the other young, growing followers of Jesus about
whom these stories were written.

Illustrations by Chris Wold Dyrud

All Scripture quotations are taken from The Living Bible, Copyright © 1971 by Tyndale House Publishers, Wheaton, Ill. Used by permission.

Published by Bethany House Publishers
A division of Bethany Fellowship, Inc.
6820 Auto Club Road, Minneapolis, Minnesota 55438

Printed in the United States of America

Library of Congress Cataloging in Publication Data

Beamer, Charles.
    Joshua Wiggins and the king's kids.

    Summary: Relates how a young Christian discovers what his faith means to him and how he can share it with others. A pertinent Bible verse and discussion questions follow each episode.
    1. Children—Prayer-books and devotions—English. [1. Christian life]
I. Wold, Christine A.,   ill.   II. Title.
BV4870.B38   248.8'2   81-10162
ISBN 0-87123-268-5   AACR2

The Author

CHARLES BEAMER is a free-lance writer and professional photographer. He has written several books and many articles. Mr. Beamer took his B.A. degree in English and History from North Texas State University and a Master's Degree in English from the University of Texas. He is married and the father of five children, ranging in age from 8 to 16. He is presently living in Denton, Texas.

Contents

Preface

In the Father's garden there are few "plants" more vulnerable to attack from within and without than new, young ones. The tendency of many parents—myself, for one—is to say, "Ah, now that my child has become a Christian, I can relax." But the parents' job is just beginning.

This book focuses on two main areas of young Christians' spiritual life: their new-found enthusiasm for Jesus Christ—and the desire to share that enthusiasm with others, and a new-found thirst to learn about and become like their Master. The family devotionals that follow give examples of young Christians learning to share their faith and learning more about their faith. Application of the examples provided by the stories depends on the diligence of you, the parent. The scripture passage and the discussion questions that follow each episode are designed to help you do the best possible job of applying the truths in this book.

The Many Secrets of Joshua Wiggins

Day 1

Shhh!

"Well, Grandpa," called Mr. Wiggins, "why don't we haul away your old Chrysler today? We've put it off long enough."

"Good idea," the white-haired, elder Wiggins replied. He stood up from his chair and put on his cap. He started to go with his son out the door.

Joshua raced into the room with a shocked look. "Dad! Grandpa! You can't—I mean, you *can't* take the old car away."

"Why not, son?" Mr. Wiggins asked.

Joshua looked sheepish. "You just *can't*, that's all."

"Oh," his father said with a knowing wink at Grandpa, "another of your secrets?"

Joshua nodded, beginning to squirm.

His father went over to him and laid a hand on Joshua's shoulder. "What is the car—your clubhouse?"

Joshua shook his head without looking at his father.

"A hideout?"

Again, Joshua shook his head. But this time he glanced up and saw the friendly twinkle in his father's eyes. He also noticed the patient way his grandfather was looking at him. Putting one forefinger to his lips, Joshua whispered, "Shhh!"

"All right," his father whispered back. "I won't tell anyone—especially not Janice."

Joshua wrinkled his face at the thought of how his older sister, Janice, teased him about his secrets. Then, leaning close to his father, he whispered, "The car's our super secret spy station."

His father nodded seriously. "So, if we hauled it away, the spies would be out of business?"

Joshua nodded.

"Couldn't the spies escape to another country or build another station?" his father asked hopefully.

Joshua looked worried. "Not yet, please. But we'll be ready to move soon, okay?"

Mr. Wiggins looked at Grandpa. Slowly he said to Joshua, "I suppose your mother could be persuaded to let it stay. We might still get around to restoring the old thing."

"The super secret spy station," Grandpa corrected, winking at Josh.

"Not too loud, Grandpa, please. Remember, it's a *secret!*" he implored.

Mr. Wiggins watched Grandpa gladly take off his cap and return to his chair. He watched Joshua's face burst into a huge smile as he ran to the telephone. Then he went to see what was next on his list of Saturday chores.

Joshua called his best friend, Chris, to tell him that the old Chrysler had been spared.

"Want to come over and play in it?" Joshua asked. "I got a new lock box we can put the secret defense plans in."

"Aw," Chris began, "I'd rather work on the secret cl—"

"Shhh!" Joshua hissed, looking around to see if his sister was nearby. In a whisper as soft as an evening breeze he added, "Can you get away without being followed?"

"Sure," Chris replied.

"See you there!"

" 'Kay."

Joshua slipped the receiver back onto the hook. He tiptoed past his grandfather's chair and slipped into his room. As quietly as he could, he found his hammer and stuck it behind his belt. Carefully he placed a handful of nails into the left front pocket of his jeans. Then, just like a cat going outside at night, he crept from his room. Within moments he had sneaked out of the house and had hidden behind the bushes at the corner. There, looking in all directions, he waited for his friend.

"[Jesus] replied, 'You are permitted to know some truths about

*the Kingdom of God that are hidden to those outside the King-
dom...'"* (Mark 4:11).

Discussion Questions:
1. Who was Joshua's best friend? What can you share with a best friend that you can't share with everyone else?
2. What "secrets" ("hidden truths") do Christians have? Are people likely to tease us about our "secrets"? What are we supposed to do with our "secrets"?
3. Have you ever felt embarrassed about being a Christian? Have you ever felt so glad about being a Christian that you wanted to tell someone else? What happened in each case?

Day 2

The Secret Clubhouse

Fields lay to the east of the Wiggins home. Beyond the fields were dark, thick woods. Past the woods were pastures where cattle grazed. To the east and south of the pastures were rows and rows of houses, some of which were still being built.

Joshua and Chris raced across the fields, following a secret path they had marked with small stones. They came to their secret crossing place through a fence and ducked into it. Then, they disappeared into the woods. They turned to see if they had been followed.

"That was close!" whispered Joshua.

"Yeah, Black Bart and his gang almost got us that time," Chris replied, wiping his forehead.

"Think it's safe to go on to the clubhouse?" Joshua asked.

Chris nodded, and the boys turned and began following a trail down into a creek bed. They edged their way around a pool of water. The surface of the pool was covered with bright yellow leaves from nearby bois d'arc trees. The boys scrambled up a steep bank and trotted into the grove of trees. Stopping at the base of the largest tree, they scanned the ground.

"No tracks," Chris observed.

Joshua smiled. "See, I told you nobody knows about this place."

Chris nodded and began climbing the tree. A few feet up, steps had been nailed to the trunk. The steps led up two main branches to a platform. The frame of a room stood at the far end of the platform. Chris pulled himself over the edge of the platform and called down, "You tie the boards we brought the other day onto the rope, and I'll pull them up."

"Okay," Joshua said, turning toward what appeared to be only a pile of leaves. He brushed aside the top leaves and uncovered several boards. A rope came whistling down from the platform, and Joshua tied two of the boards onto the end of it. He waved, and immediately the boards began jerking up into the air.

When Joshua had climbed up to the platform, he joined Chris in nailing one of the boards into place on the front of the room. He paused to fish a nail from his pocket and grinned to his friend. "It's neat having a secret clubhouse, isn't it?"

"Yeah," Chris replied. "This way, if the country ever gets into another war, we'll have a place to hide. Why, we could even sneak out from here, raid the enemy, then get back to safety!"

Joshua frowned as he began to drive the nail into the board. Quietly he said, "I hope we don't ever get into another war. Dad still talks about how bad the last one was."

Chris laughed bravely. "Aw, you just want to grow up and marry Lori; and if a war came, you couldn't."

Joshua's frown deepened. Looking at his friend, he asked, "You haven't told anybody I like her, have you?"

Chris shot him a hurt look. "As long as you don't tell the teacher who dropped that library book in the mud, I won't tell anybody about you and Lori. A deal is a deal."

Joshua nodded, satisfied. "Boy," he muttered as he struck the nail head solidly, "if Janice and her friends or the kids at school found out I like Lori..." He shook his head with a solemn look.

"A secret's a secret," Chris stated, picking up the other board, "and a friend is a friend." He started a nail into the board. "And I don't tell my friends' secrets!"

"Yes, you are my Rock and, my fortress; honor your name by leading me out of this peril. Pull me from the trap my enemies have set for me. For you alone are strong enough ... You have rescued me, O God who keeps his promises" (Ps. 31:3-5).

Discussion Questions:

1. What was the name of the "bad guy" Joshua and Chris were afraid was following them? What are the names of *your* "bad guys"?
2. Where did the boys go to hide and be protected? In the scripture quoted above, where did the Psalmist go for protection? Of all the people and places that can protect us, which is the most reliable?
3. What is a *real* friend like? What should we do with and for our friends?

Day 3

Broken Promises

At the supper table that evening, Mr. Wiggins asked Joshua to pray the blessing. But Joshua hung his head and began to squirm. "You say it," he murmured.

"It's your turn," Janice accused.

"It's not!" Joshua snapped back. "I said it—"

"Stop that!" their mother said. "The supper prayer isn't something to argue over. If you can't thank the Lord with a glad heart, then—"

"Oh, Josh's just mad 'cause everybody knows about him and *Lori*," Janice said, looking sideways at Joshua.

The look on Joshua's face was like shattered glass. Horrified, he jumped up and ran from the dining room. As his parents and grandfather wondered what had happened, he slammed the door of his room. Janice shrugged and said, "*I'll* be glad to say the prayer."

The family ate supper silently. Afterward, Mr. Wiggins sighed, "I guess I'd better go talk with him—find out what this is all about."

"No, son," Grandpa said gently. "Let *me* talk to the boy." He stared at Janice, who lowered her eyes and hastily began clearing the dishes from the supper table. "But first," Grandpa added, "I'd like to hear from big sister what the rumor is about."

Flustered, she blurted, "It's nothing much. Chris Dobbs told Sammy Fletcher that Joshua's in love with Lori; and Sammy told Wendy, who told—"

"So," Grandpa concluded, "one of Joshua's secrets has been broken."

Janice went to the sink and began washing the dishes while Grandpa went to Joshua's door. He knocked several times. When he heard no answer, he went into Joshua's room and closed the door silently behind him. The boy was lying on the bed, sobbing into his pillow.

Grandpa sat on the edge of the bed and rubbed Josh's back until he stopped crying. Then the elder Wiggins said, "Hurts, doesn't it? When a friend tells a secret, I mean."

Numbly, Joshua nodded. He sat up and wiped his cheeks.

"Do you feel like you've been stabbed in the back?"

Joshua again nodded, sniffing.

"What do you think you can do about it?" Grandpa asked.

"I hate him!" Joshua growled angrily. "I'm gonna kill him!"

Grandpa laughed gently and laid one hand on Joshua's shoulder. "What do you think Jesus would have done about this?"

Joshua stared. "What does *He* have to do with Chris breaking a promise to me?" he asked.

Grandpa's eyes had a pleasant twinkle in them. "You have a birthday coming up. Have you forgotten?"

Confused, Joshua protested, "I just *had* my birthday."

"The birthday I'm talking about will be your *first* birthday," Grandpa said, smoothing down Joshua's hair.

Josh lowered his head, frowning. "You mean the birthday of when I became a Christian?"

Grandpa nodded. "And since you're a young Christian, you may not have thought about what your new Master has to do with things like friends who break promises."

Joshua's expression changed from confusion to thoughtfulness. "Jesus would forgive Chris, wouldn't He?" he asked timidly.

Grandpa again nodded. "Do you have the courage to do that?"

Joshua squirmed. "I'd rather hit him in the mouth!"

His grandfather laughed and lifted the boy's chin with one hand. "Let me ask you something else. Does Chris know you're a Christian?"

"No," Joshua answered slowly.

"Has that been another of your secrets?"

Even more slowly, Joshua nodded.

"Josh, have you ever talked to other people about your best friend, Chris?"

"Of course," Joshua answered quickly. "But I won't anymore!"

Grandpa laid one hand on Joshua's right shoulder. "Isn't Jesus Christ not only your Master but also your friend—your very best friend you could tell other people about?"

Joshua nodded.

"And has He *ever* hurt you?"

"No," Joshua replied, "but what's that got to do with—"

"I just thought," Grandpa said, standing, "that when you forgive

Chris, you might tell him about your other best friend. Maybe he needs to know."

"He sure does!" Joshua declared—then he felt ashamed and hung his head.

"It's all right to be proud of being a Christian," Grandpa said, "but instead of judging others because they aren't, we need to share our secret."

Joshua squirmed. Reluctantly, he said, "Okay—I'll try." Then he looked up quickly. "But do you think it'll make any difference?"

"It won't wipe away the hurt you feel. Only prayer can do that. And it won't guarantee that Chris—or someone else—won't hurt you again. And it won't make your secret a secret again." He smiled and bent over to kiss Joshua on the crown of his head. "But after all, having a few people know you like a girl isn't the worst thing that could happen."

"I don't know," Joshua said with a worried look.

"Jesus replied, ' "Love the Lord your God with all your heart, soul, and mind. This is the first and greatest commandment. The second most important is similar: Love your neighbor as much as you love yourself" ' " (Matt. 22:37-39).

Discussion Questions:
1. In this episode, what decisions or choices did Joshua have to make?
2. After reading the scripture above, talk about why love is so important to Christian living. Why is Satan happy if we're angry or resentful toward other people?
3. Tell about a time when a friend hurt you. What did you feel like doing about it? What *did* you do about it? What does the Bible say you could have done?

16

Day 4

The Battle

What am I going to do? thought Joshua, squirming under his covers in bed that night. He was still *mad* at Chris—and Janice. And he was embarrassed to death that everyone knew about his feelings for Lori! But more powerful than those feelings was the feeling that made him terribly afraid to mention—to anyone, much less to Chris—that he was a Christian. Why couldn't he just keep it a secret? Why did he have to *tell* anybody?

"I can't ask Chris to go to church," Joshua said to himself. "His parents won't let him even go to Bible Club, much less to the services. And besides, what good would it do?" Anger against Chris rose up inside him, drowning all his other thoughts.

Then he remembered what his mother had told him not long before he had become a Christian: "Inside you and all around you, there is a voice of the darkness and there is a voice of the light fighting for you. Many, *many* times you'll have to decide which voice you want to obey."

He tried to close out the voice whispering to him to be angry, to remember all the other times friends had hurt him and betrayed his secrets. But he couldn't stop listening. The whispering voice made him feel more and more frustrated. Then he recalled that his grandfather had once told him, "When you're troubled, that's the time to pray—and keep on praying!" He was worn out from worrying and being angry. Now he found it easy to pray—and wished he had done so earlier, before the whispering voice had reminded him of so many bad things.

The next thing he knew, it was morning. It was Sunday, and he felt good—until he remembered that somehow he had to deal with Chris. They had agreed to meet at the secret clubhouse at one o'clock. That meant he had little more than five hours to figure out what to do!

17

In silence Joshua sweated through Sunday school and the main service. In confusion he sweated through lunch, then slipped outside and ran across the fields. It felt good to run like the wind across the open land, and he wished he could just keep running.

He climbed up to the clubhouse and sat down to wait. With his heart beating fast, he thought about Chris. A gentle voice reminded him of all the fun he'd had with Chris—the "battles" they'd fought and won, the "enemies" they'd killed or driven into the wilderness. *But,* Joshua thought grimly, *Chris stabbed me in the back! He told!*

He was startled by a voice. " 'Lo," said Chris, climbing up with his usual stealth. "Been waiting long?"

Joshua blinked at him as though awakening. "No, not long," he said.

Chris stood near the edge of the platform. "What'cha doing?"

Joshua sighed. "Just sitting here, wishing you hadn't told anyone about Lori and me." He looked up at Chris.

Chris bristled. "I didn't, and whoever told you that is a—"

"It's okay," Joshua said, holding up one hand. "I—forgive you."

"Well, that's big of you!" Chris huffed, stalking to the room at the end of the platform. He turned and glared at Joshua. "Who needs your forgiveness anyhow?" He kicked at the boards they'd nailed on the room the day before. "I didn't *mean* to tell anyone your secret. It—it just slipped out when Sammy asked me if you liked her."

Joshua listened in disbelief, thinking, *I'm the one who should be mad! Why is he so upset?* He forced himself to keep silent.

Seeing Joshua's calm look, Chris lowered his gaze and kicked the boards again. "You can stare at me all you want to," he muttered, "but all I can say is—is that I'm sorry!" He looked at the bois d'arc fruit rotting on the bare ground below and wished he could chunk the grapefruit-sized balls at a cow or something. "I mean, just because you're perfect..."

"What?" Joshua stammered. "I don't think I'm perfect at all!"

Chris scuffed the platform with the tip of one shoe. "I just mean—well, *you* don't hurt people. So, I'm sorry I told your secret." With a worried look, he added, "You won't tell the teacher I ruined the book, will you?"

Joshua shook his head and stood. Looking down at the rotting yellow fruit, he remembered that a year before when the fruit first began to fall from the trees, Chris had been afraid to pick one of them up. Someone had told him they were poisonous, so he had been afraid even to touch one. Then Joshua began to recall other things: Chris was afraid of the cattle in the pastures beyond the woods; he even was afraid of the woods when night came. And Chris, Joshua remembered, was the one who had made up Black Bart and his gang of thieves and cutthroats—and really seemed afraid when they played like they were being chased by the gang. So, maybe Chris *did* need to know about Joshua's *other* best friend! Joshua took a deep breath—and felt as if he were about to make a high dive into a swimming pool.

" *'Try to show as much compassion as your Father does.'* "
" *'Love your enemies. Do good to those who hate you. Pray for the happiness of those who curse you; implore God's blessing on those who hurt you.'* "
" *'Don't be afraid! Just trust [Jesus]'* " (Luke 6:36, 27-28; 8:50).

Discussion Questions:
1. In this chapter, what was Chris afraid of? What was Joshua afraid of? What feeling (emotion) most often stops us from doing things that Jesus Christ wants us to do? How can we defeat that feeling?
2. How is it possible to love our enemies: by feelings (emotions) or by choice (will)?
3. Tell what you would say to Chris if you were Joshua. What would you do if Chris laughed at you? What would you do if Chris said he wanted to know more about your "other best friend"?

Day 5

The Dive

Joshua took another deep breath and made his "dive." "Chris," he began, "I want you to meet my *other* best friend."

Chris looked at him with curiosity, and Joshua continued, "He's a friend who won't ever, *ever* hurt you. He'll see that your needs get met—especially when you need love. And, best of all, he won't ever, *ever* make you afraid. In fact, if you let Him, he can make you so you won't be afraid of *anything!*"

Chris laughed slightly. "He's not like Black Bart, huh?"

Joshua shook his head. "Not at all."

Chris grinned and sat on the platform. "Is He another of your secrets? I mean, I didn't know you had *another* best friend."

Joshua frowned. "I should have told you sooner—but you know how I am about secrets." He erased his frown and added, "Anyhow, this friend of mine isn't a secret. Or He shouldn't be, that is." He paused to pray, looking off at the rounded tops of the trees, the clear blue sky, and the warm, bright sunlight.

"Well?" Chris asked impatiently. "Are you going to tell me?"

Joshua looked at his friend's eager brown eyes and said, "His name is Jesus Christ. He's the Son of God—and the Master of my life."

As he told Chris about how he had confessed his sins and asked Jesus to take over his life, Joshua was surprised at how easy it was to tell about the "secret." In fact, he felt greatly relieved and glad to tell this secret because as his own joy bubbled up, it spread to Chris, who began smiling.

When they finally climbed down from the tree house, Joshua stopped by the trunk and said, "You know, for once we *really* whipped Black Bart."

"What?" Chris asked, laughing.

Joshua began walking toward home. "He lost a *real* fight today, that's all."

Joining in the game as he hurried after Joshua, Chris asked, "But he and his gang will be back, won't they?"

"Sure," Joshua called, beginning to run, "but with the friend I told you about on our side, we don't have to worry! Some day, Black Bart and all his men will be dead."

"But we won't be?"

"But we won't be!"

Together, the friends raced each other across the fields with the dazzling sunshine before them.

"If anyone publicly acknowledges me as his friend, I will openly acknowledge him as my friend before my Father in heaven. But if anyone publicly denies me, I will openly deny him before my Father in heaven."

"... don't worry about what to say at your trial, for you will be given the right words at the right time. For it won't be you doing the talking—it will be the Spirit of your heavenly Father speaking through you!" (Matt. 10:32-33; 19-20).

Discussion Questions:
1. Why did Joshua pray before telling Chris about Jesus Christ?
2. Why do you think Joshua said Black Bart "lost a *real* fight"?
3. What are some of the fights *you* won after you gave your life to Jesus Christ?

WEEK TWO

Chris's Dove

Day 1

It's My Life

"No, you may *not* go back to church with Joshua Wiggins!" Chris's mother said angrily. "And you certainly may not be baptized!" She glared down at Chris, her arms folded.

"You don't care what happens to me!" Chris protested as loudly as he dared. He was close to tears, but he fought them back.

"I most certainly do!" his mother answered, leaning close to him.

"You don't! You don't care if I'm protected or not!"

She stared at her son, then suddenly laughed. More quietly, she said, "Chris, *we* protect you."

Chris pouted, turning away. "I don't know what difference it makes to you if I'm baptized. It's *my* life."

His mother grabbed him by one shoulder and turned him around. "Neither your father nor I believe that religion does anyone any good!"

"You ought to!" Chris said.

"Well, it certainly hasn't done *you* any good. You sass me just as much as ever. You get into just as much trouble at school. And you seem to be angry *all* the time!" She folded her arms again and glared at him.

Chris started to walk away. "Sure, blame everything on me. Dad's always away flying. You're always busy working or taking care of Emilie and Randy. And everything bad that happens is *my* fault!" He turned and glared hatefully at his mother. "If I'm so bad, why don't you put me in jail?"

23

She softened and tried to put one hand on his shoulder. But he ran to the door and jerked it open. "I hate you!" he screamed. "I hate you, and I don't want to live with you! I'll *show* you whose fault everything is!"

With that, he slammed the door and disappeared at a run. His mother followed him, but by the time she got to the yard, he was gone.

"When someone becomes a Christian he becomes a brand new person inside. He is not the same any more. A new life has begun!" (2 Cor. 5:17).

Discussion Questions:
1. What reasons did Chris's mother have for saying that religion hadn't done him any good?
2. How do you know if *you* really are a Christian—a follower of the Lord Jesus Christ?
3. When becoming a Christian (a "little Christ"), a person prays once to receive Jesus into his heart. Is there more to do after this? (See Matthew 5:48.)

Take THAT!

Hurt deeply, Chris stumbled along a sidewalk as fast as he could. He didn't care—and really didn't see—where he was going. All he knew was that he had to get away—far away! He felt cornered. He felt condemned. He had tried to do things right, but everything always turned out wrong. He *wanted* to do right. He *wanted* to please his mother and father. And he *wanted* to please Jesus Christ and be His friend. But it seemed no matter what he did, it turned out wrong! Crying, he grabbed a rock and hurled it down the street, not caring what it hit.

It whacked a car coming toward him. The driver slammed on his brakes and jumped out. "Hey! Hey, kid! You come back here!"

But Chris was already across two yards, running as fast as he could. Unfortunately, he was cutting across a beautifully-kept lawn with his head down; he didn't see Mr. Clardy watering his rosebushes.

"Say you, boy! Didn't you see my sign: 'Don't walk on the grass'? Can't you kids read?" shouted Mr. Clardy, running toward Chris with the hose still spraying. Chris thought he was going to be soaked or hit with the hose. He raced from the yard and cut across the street.

Brakes squealed; tires screeched. A car slid to a stop not five feet from the frightened boy.

A block away, Chris slowed his pace and dutifully stayed on the sidewalk. He stamped on every crack he came to. He named each crack he stamped: "Take *that*, Mother! Take *that*, Daddy! Take *that*, Emilie! Take *that*, Randy! Take *that*, Mr. Clardy!" He almost stamped a crack and said, "Take *that*, God!" But he didn't.

After all, what Joshua had told him about God and Jesus Christ *had* worked—for a while. For a while Chris knew he had felt at peace. For a while he had felt *right.* But now it seemed that even God had turned against him. *Everything* had gone wrong. Everyone was mad at him, and he couldn't do anything right!

25

Chris glanced toward the blue sky above the sycamore trees along the sidewalk. "God?" he asked silently. "Why are you mad at me? Am I such a bad person? What did I do to make you punish me? I tried to be good, but I..." He could think of a dozen or more reasons why the "bad" things had happened. He hadn't *meant* to talk in class and get sent to the principal's office. He hadn't *meant* to push Emilie so hard that she fell and skinned her knees. He hadn't *meant* to keep his mother mad at him all the time. It just seemed like the harder he tried to do things right, the more they went wrong.

Take the business of being baptized, for instance. After talking with Joshua and Josh's pastor, Chris had known that he wanted to be saved. He had asked Jesus into his heart; he had accepted Him as the Lord of his life. And he had wanted to be baptized to show that he had died to sin. He had felt sure his mother and father not only would be pleased, but would be very happy for his decision. So, when they had gotten mad at him, he had been shocked—and hurt. And he couldn't understand their anger.

Now, he wanted to chuck it all. He guessed he had made a mistake in trying to be a Christian. He guessed he should have just stayed like he was—a quiet kid who never did or said much of anything. At least when he was quiet and didn't do much, he stayed out of trouble.

Then a voice inside said to him, "Everyone thinks you're such a bad kid, you might as well really become one!" He smiled. It was a sad smile, but he did his best to make it a mean, tough smile.

He saw that he was near the drive-in grocery store a block from his school—the school he was skipping for the day. He went into the store as quietly as he could. The manager was busy checking in a shipment. Chris sneaked around two counters to the candy rack and began slipping packages of gum and candy into his jeans pockets. When he had filled both pockets, he took a deep breath to calm his pounding heart. Then he headed for the door.

Just as he was about to go out, a truant officer in a gray uniform came in. The large man blocked Chris's way, glaring down at him. "Which school are you supposed to be in?" demanded the officer.

Chris tried to worm his way past the man, but he moved with Chris, keeping him inside. The store manager looked up curiously, then began to frown. "Say, what's making your pockets bulge out? Have you been shoplifting?"

Chris looked from the truant officer to the store manager. He tried to make a run for it, but the officer grabbed him by both shoulders. The man said to the manager, "You'd better call the police."

26

"In a race, everyone runs but only one person gets first prize. So run your race to win. To win the contest you must deny yourselves many things that would keep you from doing your best. An athlete goes to all this trouble just to win a blue ribbon or a silver cup, but we do it for a heavenly reward that never disappears" (1 Cor. 9:24-25).

Discussion Questions:
1. What reasons did Chris have for skipping school and shoplifting? Would he have been better off if he had "gotten away with it"?
2. Who was trying to keep Chris from winning his "race"? How was he trying to "trip him up"? Why?
3. What do you think Paul meant by saying he knew we must deny ourselves in order to do our best?

Day 3

"I'm Sorry"

Chris must've said "I'm sorry" a hundred or more times in the next few days. But it did very little good.

The police came to the store. Two policemen, the truant officer, and the store manager all gathered around him. They questioned him and questioned him. Chris could do little more than cry and say, "I'm sorry."

The police took him to the police station. A social worker came from the county office. Chris was talked to ... and talked to ... and talked to. Finally the social worker telephoned his mother. When she came to claim her son, Chris again cried, "I'm sorry!" Over and over during the ride home, he repeated it. But his mother only stared grimly ahead.

When she got home, she made him go to the hackberry tree in the backyard and cut a switch. Then she spanked him with the switch. But worse than the spanking was the fact that she wouldn't speak to him. She wouldn't accept his apologies or his attempts to make up. He was sent to his room. The rest of the day he spent crying on his bed.

When his father came home that night—still wearing his pilot's uniform—he and Chris's mother talked in their room for a long time. Then Chris's father came and had a serious talk with Chris. The talk ended with his father getting furious and yelling, "You're grounded for the rest of the school year! No phone calls, no playing—nothing but study! Do you understand me?" Chris quietly nodded. He was glad he hadn't gotten another whipping, but he was sorry his father hadn't listened to him.

Not that Chris knew exactly what to say; he was too confused. All he knew for sure was that he had failed—again. And he felt he had failed miserably. He also felt sure his parents never would forgive him or forget his crime. His younger brother and sister—Emilie and

Randy—felt the same way. They treated him like he was covered with garbage.

At school the following day, however, Chris was treated in two ways. The teachers looked at him as though he were some kind of wild animal who might jump up and kill someone at any second. But several of the kids treated Chris as something of a hero. "You got *arrested*?" several kids asked him. "Gosh, did the police *beat* you or anything?"

At first, Chris felt better being a "hero." The tough boys paid him compliments. The biggest compliment came when they invited him to join the "Scorpions" club. But the nice kids avoided him. In fact, they stood around in small groups on the playground, whispering and pointing toward him. Even Janie Warren—the girl he liked—snubbed him. When he tried to talk with her, she ran away as though he had blood dripping from his hands. Chris was crushed.

On the way home from school, Chris was dragging along by himself when he heard someone yell, "Hey, Chris, wait up!" He turned and saw Joshua running to catch him. He felt like hiding.

"What's wrong?" Joshua asked.

"You haven't heard?" Chris asked, amazed.

Joshua shrugged. "Sure, I've heard what everybody's saying. But I wanted to ask *you*. I thought we were friends."

Chris gave Josh a doubtful look. "Can you be friends with a criminal?"

"If Jesus could be friends with 'bad' people, so can I," Josh said, "'cause I'm not exactly perfect, either." He paused, then asked, "Have you prayed about what happened?"

Chris looked at him as though Josh had asked him if he had tried sticking his hand into a meat grinder. "God's probably mad at me, too."

"Have you asked Him to forgive you?"

Chris felt like crying, but he merely shook his head. "He wouldn't."

"Come on," he said. "Let's pray about it."

Chris looked at Josh, amazed. "Where?" he asked.

"Right here, while we're walking home."

Chris felt embarrassed. He looked around, undecided.

"Look," Joshua said, "why do you think God sent Jesus, His Son, to die here on earth?"

"He died—for our sins. Your Sunday school teacher read us that."

"And what's more," Joshua said, "if Jesus hadn't come, God *would* be mad at you. But Grandpa says that Jesus opened up a new way for us to get to God. Jesus is in heaven right now. He's telling God, 'Don't be mad at Chris; he wants to be a good kid, and we've got to help him.' "

Chris's eyes widened. He wanted to believe it was true—but something inside kept trying to tell him that it couldn't be true. Josh saw the look in Chris's eyes and figured out what he was thinking.

"Chris, would Jesus lie to you?"

"No!" Chris quickly replied.

"Well, in the Bible Jesus said that we should pray, 'Forgive us our sins, just as we have forgiven those who have sinned against us.' "*

Chris stopped. He felt as if someone had just opened a door in front of him. "You mean, God will forgive me, and I have to forgive people who have done me wrong?"

Joshua nodded. "That way, we get rid of *all* our bad feelings. God doesn't want us carrying around stuff like anger and guilt. If we carry those feelings around inside us, we can't do what God wants us to. And Satan can get to us real easily if we're mad or hurt all the time."

Another "door" opened in front of Chris. "You mean, if I've been mad at other people, Satan can use that to make me do bad things?"

"Satan can't *make* you do anything. It's always your choice."

"Oh," Chris said weakly, walking on. Soon he asked, "Josh, what does God want me to do?"

Joshua grinned. "Ask for forgiveness, forgive other people—and yourself, too. And don't forget, God loves you!"

—

"Then Peter came to him and asked, 'Sir, how often should I forgive a brother who sins against me? Seven times?'

" 'No!' Jesus replied, 'seventy times seven!' " (Matt. 18:21-22).

Discussion Questions:
1. How did different people treat Chris after they found out about his crime? Why do you suppose the different people treated him in the ways they did?
2. What is the difference between *being* forgiven and *feeling* forgiven?
3. Seventy times seven equals 490, but what do you think Jesus really meant in the scripture quoted above? What is a "forgiving heart" or a "forgiving attitude"?

---
*Matthew 6:12

30

Day 4

Thinking

Thinking was not one of Chris's favorite activities. He would much rather have been out running, playing baseball, exploring a creek with Joshua, or building something. But he was grounded, so he couldn't do any of his favorite things after school. Instead, he lay on his bed in his room. And he did a lot of thinking.

He also did a lot of praying. He wasn't too sure how to go about it, so he got started by finding the prayer Josh had said was in the Bible: the Lord's Prayer. He understood it well enough to make a beginning. But he still wasn't sure he was getting through to God. After all, he couldn't see God, and God certainly didn't see fit to speak directly to him. So, Chris wondered frequently if God had even heard him.

Bit by bit, day by day, he did feel better. That is, he felt less guilty about what he had done. Also, he was convinced that he never would commit a crime again—even if he could get away with it. And he made up his mind that never again did he want to feel like he was garbage. He decided that even if no one else in the world liked him, he at least had to like himself.

And he did. Even if his parents did seem to be mad at him a lot, he knew he really was a pretty good kid. And even if his teachers did think he was a problem, he knew inside whether or not he was *trying* to do his best. But much more than those thoughts was one that grew and grew inside him: God did love him.

He figured that out by reading the Bible. What he figured out was something like this: If God hadn't loved everyone, including Chris Dobbs, He wouldn't have sent His Son to die a horrible, painful death so that people could be forgiven their sins and come back to God. Chris cried when he read how Jesus had died. And as he cried, he said over and over, "I'm sorry, God. I'm sorry I messed things up!"

Then the question came to him: What was he going to do about it? He couldn't stay in his room forever. He couldn't keep his mouth

31

shut and his hands in his pockets forever either. Josh had said that God wanted him to love others. Did that mean loving them even when they were mean, even when they did unfair things? Chris guessed it did.

But how was he to stop himself from getting mad when people were mean or unfair? How could he keep Satan from making him burn with anger and run off or tear things up? Chris laughed. He guessed he'd just have to pray about that, too. And pray hard, since it seemed to be a hard problem for him. He sighed and flopped backwards onto his bed. His right hand fell onto his Bible, and he patted it. He'd just have to do it, that's all! *Because,* he thought, *if God loves me—and He does—then how can I treat other people in any other way than with love?*

He began by smiling at his mother.

His mother looked suspiciously at him. "What are you grinning about?" she asked. "Have you done something else you're afraid you'll get into trouble for?"

Anger welled up inside Chris, and he felt like running into his room and crying. A voice screamed inside his head, "See? They even accuse you of doing bad when you're trying to do good! It's not fair!"

Chris swallowed hard and smiled again. "I just love you, that's all."

His mother blinked, staring at him. Her expression softened. Suddenly, she laughed gently and hugged him.

From then on, things became easier. Chris smiled at his father the next time his father came home. His father asked, "What do you want?"

Chris said, "Nothing. I just love you, that's all."

His father tilted his head slightly to one side. "Oh," he said mildly. "Well, I love you, too, Chris." He patted his son on his head and went to sit and read the newspaper.

"Can I do anything for you?" Chris asked.

His father looked at him for several seconds as though trying to figure out if he was serious. Then he said, "You can sweep the front porch and sidewalk. That would help."

"Okay," Chris said and ran off to get a broom.

While he was sweeping, a sneaking voice in his head began whispering, "Dummy! Why should you have to be the one to *crawl* to them? *They* were the ones who misjudged you! They were the ones who—"

"Shut up, Satan," Chris muttered, sweeping harder. The voice

32

sneaked back again in a few minutes. Chris stopped sweeping, squeezed his eyes shut, and prayed, "HELP! Please, God, I need HELP!"

The voice went away. And, oddly enough, the job of sweeping—which Chris always had disliked—was finished before he knew it.

"It is true that I am an ordinary, weak human being, but I don't use human plans and methods to win my battles. I use God's mighty weapons, not those made by men, to knock down the devil's strongholds" (2 Cor. 10:3-4).

Discussion Questions:
1. In this chapter, what was Chris's "battle"? Who won? How did they win? Will there be other "battles" like this one?
2. What is "worldly" love? What is Christian love? (Read 1 Corinthians 13:4-13 for Paul's explanation of what love is.) What do you think Chris Dobbs has learned about love so far?
3. What kinds of things make it hard to love others—even people in your own family?

Day 5

Chris's Dove

That summer, Chris's Aunt Lydia gave him a most unusual gift for his birthday: a white dove in a bamboo cage. When she gave it to him, she kissed him and said, "I thought you two might get along."

Chris was thrilled—and puzzled. He had never been allowed to have a pet, so he was thrilled. But how was he supposed to play with a dove? He fed it and watered it each day. He talked to it and sat watching it each night. But he couldn't really play with it, so before very long he lost interest in it—until one day when Joshua was visiting him.

That day, Chris decided to take the dove outside and really play with it. He set the cage on the ground and took the dove out. He was holding it gently against his chest so Joshua could pet it. Then his younger brother and sister came up. Randy reached for the bird, but Chris angrily yelled, "Don't touch it! It's mine!"

The dove struggled out of his hands and flew into a nearby tree.

"Now see what you've done?" Chris stormed, glaring at Randy.

"I didn't do it!" Randy protested. "You're the one who scared it by yelling." Pouting, he led Emilie back into the house.

Chris and Joshua spent the rest of the day trying to coax the dove out of the tree. Chris tried calling to it, pleading with it, even threatening it. Then he offered it a pie plate of bird seed. But the dove refused to come down from the tree.

After Joshua went home and after supper that night, Chris tried again to get the dove to come back to him. But it turned its head to one side and cooed sadly. Chris at last gave up in frustration and sat down in the yard. He began to cry.

"It's just like everything else," he muttered, slinging a handful of grass. "I want to do what's right, but everything I do turns out wrong!" He looked toward the vast nighttime sky and stared at the twinkling stars through his tears.

Why, he wondered, had Aunt Lydia given him a dove anyhow?

Why couldn't she have given him a dog or a pet snake? He sighed and lay back on the grass, gradually growing calmer. *Maybe,* he thought, *maybe she was trying to tell me something. After all, she did say, "I thought you two might get along."* He grew calmer, thinking about how he was like the dove—or wanted to be. But before he could think further, he heard a soft rustle of wings. He looked and saw the dove fanning the air as it settled onto his chest.

He grinned as the bird shuffled its feathers into place. "Hello," he whispered.

The dove cooed.

Slowly, Chris sat upright, making no move to grab at the dove. It eyed him, then climbed up his chest and onto his left shoulder. He felt its warmth by his face. Leaning his head over, he touched the dove's softness against his cheek. "You love me, don't you?" Chris murmured.

The dove cooed, nestling down onto Chris's shirt.

He never forgot the dove's soft warmth. He began to understand why his aunt had given him such a pet.

Later that summer, his parents suggested that he be baptized. And a few months after that, they, too, became followers of Jesus Christ.

"*'I am sending you out as sheep among wolves. Be as wary as serpents and harmless as doves.'*" (Matt. 10:16).

Discussion Questions:

1. What did Chris learn about love from his pet dove? What do you think he understood about why his Aunt Lydia gave him such a pet?
2. What do you think Jesus meant by telling His disciples to be "wary as serpents and harmless as doves"?
3. How has Chris changed? How do you suppose he will treat his other friends—like Janie Warren?

WEEK THREE

Night Fears

Day 1

I'm NOT Afraid!

"What's Dotty Jensen got that I don't?" Janie Warren asked Richard, the boy she liked.

Richard grinned and glanced toward a bunch of boys on the playground who were watching him. Squinting, he turned back to Janie and whispered, "Well, for one thing, *she'll* go with me to see *Terror in the Streets* and you won't!" With a half grin, he turned and went back to his gang—the Scorpions.

Janie sighed and frowned as she turned away. Slowly she returned to her group of friends—the club of girls called the Fraidy Cats. The club's president, Denise Kibler, was first to speak to her.

"Did he ask you to go with him?"

Looking at the bare dirt of the playground, Janie shook her head. "No," she muttered.

"Why?" Denise asked, sneering slightly as she glanced at the other Fraidy Cats. " 'Cause you won't go to *Terror in the Streets* with him?"

Janie gave Denise a hard look, wondering how she had known. "My parents won't let me go," she protested.

"Ours won't either," Denise said easily. "But that's why we're the Fraidy Cats, 'cause *we're* not afraid of *anything* or *anybody!*"

Janie squirmed slightly. "It's an 'R' rated movie, Denise. My parents said they don't want me seeing things like that."

" 'Fraidy cat, 'fraidy cat!" Denise jeered, laughing. Several of the other girls laughed with her, and Janie's ears began to burn.

"I'm *not* afraid!" she insisted. "I just don't want to get caught."

"The movie's at the Cinema 4," Denise said easily. "We're going to buy tickets to one of the other shows—one of those dumb old 'PG' rated kiddy things—then slip into 'Terror.' No one'll catch us. Besides, do you want to go with Richard or not?"

Janie nibbled her lower lip as she looked toward the boys' gang. Richard was the nicest looking boy in her class, and he was one of the "in" boys—like she was one of the "in" girls. She frowned, thinking that it just wasn't fair for her parents *always* to try to keep her from doing the things her friends were doing!

"All right," she said quietly. "I'll go."

"Good for you!" Denise said loudly. "Now go tell Richard."

That evening after supper, Janie went into the den where her mother and father were sitting. They were watching a popular television show, and Janie had to clear her throat to get their attention. "May I go over to Denise Kibler's and study for a couple of hours?" Since she had lied to her parents in the past, this lie was easier than the first ones. Her mother glanced back at the television.

"If you'll wait until a commercial, I'll take you," she said.

"Mo-ther!" Janie protested. "It's only two blocks. I'll be careful."

"All right, dear," her mother said, looking briefly away from the television. "Study hard."

"I will," Janie said, taking a notebook and a textbook as she ran out of the house.

"If we will never live again after we die, then we might as well go and have ourselves a good time: let us eat, drink, and be merry. What's the difference? For tomorrow we die, and that ends everything! Don't be fooled by those who say such things. If you listen to them you will start acting like them. Get some sense and quit your sinning" (1 Cor. 15:32b-34a).

Discussion Questions:
1. What reasons or arguments did Janie have in favor of doing what Denise and Richard wanted her to do? From whom do you think those reasons and arguments came?
2. Look up the fifth commandment (either Ex. 20:12 or Deut. 5:16). In what ways do you think Janie would have been happier and more at peace with herself if she had obeyed that commandment? This question is a "toughie": What connection is there between the promise given with the fifth commandment and the scripture quoted above?

3. If Jesus Christ had been standing with Janie while she was talking to Denise and Richard, what would He have said to her?

Day 2

"Terror in the Streets"

In a few minutes, Janie met Denise and several more of the Fraidy Cats at a street corner near the shopping center.

"What're the books for?" Denise asked, frowning.

Janie shrugged. "I told my parents I was going to study with you."

Denise laughed. "Mine don't care where I go," she said. "Dump the books somewhere and come on!"

Janie hid her books behind a large sign and hurried to keep up with her friends. Her heart was beating fast, and she felt the palms of her hands beginning to sweat. "I hope we don't get caught," she whispered.

"Oh, don't be dumb," Denise sneered. "Only dumb kids—like Chris—get caught."

One of the other girls looked at Janie. "Chris used to like you, didn't he?"

Janie shrugged, remembering how hurt Chris had been when she had snubbed him after he had gotten into trouble for stealing.

"Boy," the fourth Fraidy Cat laughed, "haven't Chris and Joshua gotten *weird*? Going to church all the time and everything." She and the other Fraidy Cats looked at Janie.

Janie laughed with them. "Yeah," she said, "pretty weird."

Some of the boys in the Scorpions met them outside the theater. Since the boys were embarrassed to be seen with "dates," they agreed to buy tickets separately and go into the show ahead of the girls. Denise collected the girls' money, bought four tickets, and led her friends inside. They watched how the boys got into the "R" rated picture, then they did the same. It seemed so easy—and so much fun—fooling the ushers that Janie began to laugh.

Her laughter quickly died when the show began. Even Richard, who was proud of being a tough guy, jumped and turned away when the first bloody thing happened on the screen. Janie tried to close her

40

eyes, but Denise poked her ribs to make her look. On and on it went—things Janie never had imagined, things she never *wanted* to imagine. By the time it was over, she felt weak and sick.

The crowd around her, though, seemed to have enjoyed the show. As they all were pushing and jostling their way out, Janie heard young men joking to their dates. "Man, did'ja see the way—" one was exclaiming when he bumped into another man. The second man turned and said something awful, and a fight started. Janie and the other children ran for the exit. Behind them, people were yelling and fighting as ushers ran in.

Outside, Denise and several of the other kids began laughing, retelling parts of the movie. Janie looked at them, wondering what on earth they had seen that was funny! To her, it was anything but funny. She looked at the dark shadows beyond the parking lot lights, wondering if things like what she saw in the movie really did happen.

She wondered more and more about the movie becoming real as she walked home by herself. The dark streets that she never in her life had been afraid of now seemed filled with danger. Each deep shadow hid some horror. She began to run.

When she burst into her house, she almost ran head-on into her father. "Where have you been?" he demanded. "Your grandmother called to say that Grandpa is very sick and we should come help. When we called Denise's house to tell you, Denise's mother said she didn't know where you were."

Angrily, he looked down at her. "Well? Where were you?"

"Don't just pretend that you love others, really love them."
"Hate what is wrong. Stand on the side of the good."
"Don't let evil get the upper hand but conquer evil by doing good" (Rom. 12: 9, 21).

Discussion Questions:

1. How did the movie make Janie feel? How did it make the others feel? What can you add to the question from yesterday: "In what ways do you think Janie would have been happier and more at peace with herself if she had obeyed her parents?"

2. Has anyone in this story thus far done any part of what Paul urges us to do in the scripture quoted above? What differences has that fact made?

3. If you were Janie's father, what would you do now?

4. The command to "really love" has been broken several times in this chapter. List those times.

41

Day 3

Rumors

"We went for a walk," Janie lamely told her father.

Her father obviously was too concerned about his own father being sick to question her explanation. He grumbled something and called his wife. She came into the room, saw Janie, and sighed with relief.

"We were so worried," her mother said. "We were about to go looking for you, when—"

Her father sighed noisily, and her mother hurried with him to the door. She looked back at Janie and said, "We may be late getting home. You keep the doors locked—and don't go out again!"

"Yes, ma'am," Janie said meekly, watching them leave. She hurried to the door to make sure it was locked. Trembling, she watched their car disappear down the dark street.

That night was the longest in Janie's life. She sat watching television until the stations all went off. Then she played the radio—but still fear crept in on her. When she finally went to bed, the fear followed her into bed. Each sound became someone breaking into the house. Janie jumped up several times, calling, "Who's there?" When no one answered, her fears became worse than ever.

In the darkness of her room, scenes from the movie kept replaying themselves over and over in her imagination. Even when she kept her eyes wide open, the technicolor scenes kept coming—and coming. She began to cry, and she cried herself to sleep.

The next day at school, Janie was almost too tired to notice anything. Her teacher had to ask her one question three times before she heard it. On the playground, though, Janie did notice something. She noticed several girls whispering behind their hands and looking at her. She frowned, wondering if the fear from the night before showed on her face somehow. She went quickly to the bathroom to look at herself in a mirror. What she saw was her tired but normal, very pretty face—only just then she didn't think she was at all pretty. As she was leaving, two girls pushed open the door. The only thing Janie heard them say was, ". . . and now *everyone's* talking about her!"

They stopped talking when they saw Janie, and Janie hurried past them. She was certain they had been talking about her. But why?

After school, she found Denise and the other Fraidy Cats to walk home with as usual. But Denise wouldn't even look at her. Naturally, none of the other Fraidy Cats would either. Janie was on the verge of tears. She hastened in front of Denise and the other girls and demanded, "All right; what's going on?"

"With what?" Denise asked casually.

"You know with what!" Janie cried, swabbing tears off her cheeks.

One of the other girls glanced at her friends, then asked Janie in a low voice, "Is it true?"

"Is *what* true?" Janie asked, puzzled and hurt.

The girl again glanced at her friends, then said to Janie, "What Dotty Jensen is telling everyone you did with Richard."

"I didn't do *anything* with Richard!" Janie declared. Her frown deepened when her friends smirked to one another. "What's she saying?"

"Oh—nothing," Denise said with a knowing smile.

Janie felt like her whole world had turned upside down. The streets and the home where she had felt safe the day before were now places of fear. The friends she had trusted were suddenly her enemies. And the boy she had liked was now. . . "Wait'll I get my hands on Dotty Jensen," Janie muttered angrily. Then she saw that the others had gone on without her. "Hey, wait up!" she called. She hurried to catch them.

They crossed several streets, not once looking at Janie. She began to cry. She stopped. "I thought—we were friends!" she called.

Denise turned, and the others turned with her. "Janie Warren, it serves you right. I always thought you were a snob—like you were too pretty for the rest of us. So this just serves you right!" She and the other Fraidy Cats turned away as one and continued toward their homes.

By the time her parents came home from work, Janie felt like an old dishrag that had been thrown into the trash. She sat dejectedly on her bed. She was so depressed that she did not hear her father phoning his mother at the hospital to find out how Grandpa was. She did not even hear her mother in the kitchen beginning to prepare supper. All she could hear was her imagination—repeating the rumors she thought might be spreading about her; it also was replaying scenes from the movie the night before. She jumped from her bed when her father came into her room and spoke to her.

"In case you're interested," he began sourly, "which apparently you're not, my father had a heart attack. I'm glad to report, though, that he's expected to recover." He stood glaring at her. "What's the matter? Feeling guilty?"

Janie sat up on her bed and wiped her eyes. "No—sir."

"Where were you last night?" he asked firmly.

"Daddy..." she began. Her face twisted into a look of pain.

"Don't try to lie out of it," he said, sighing as he pulled a chair to her bed and sat looking at her with one eyebrow raised. "Oh, you didn't know we knew that you've lied to us in the past?"

She felt as if she was about to be pushed over a cliff. "Daddy, please...!" When she saw that his expression didn't soften, she sighed and hung her head. "We went to a movie."

"Which movie?"

"*Terror in the Streets.*"

He leaned forward angrily. "That—that horror thing we expressly told you you were not to see?"

"But, Daddy, all the other kids—"

He stood, fists on his waist. "I don't care if the whole world was going. That doesn't make it right for you to disobey!"

She slumped lower onto her bed.

When she said nothing, her father yelled, "You're grounded until further notice, and your allowance is something you can *forget!* Now get into the kitchen and help your mother, you ungrateful little rebel!"

She could stand it no further. Angrily, she stood and declared, "If you'd ever get out from in front of the television and talk...!"

He grabbed her arm, turned her around and spanked her; with the final spank he sent her toward the kitchen—crying her eyes out.

"Honor Christ by submitting to each other."
"Children, obey your parents; this is the right thing to do because God has placed them in authority over you.... And now a word to you parents. Don't keep on scolding and nagging your children, making them angry and resentful. Rather, bring them up with the loving discipline the Lord himself approves, with suggestions and godly advice" (Eph. 5:21; 6:1-2a, 4).

Discussion Questions:
1. Which one of Janie's problems do you think hurt her the most? What could she do about it?

2. What did Paul, when he was writing to the Christians at Ephesus, mean by saying they should "submit to each other"? What does "submit to each other" have to do with "love each other"? (See 1 Corinthians 13:5.) If both Janie and her father obeyed the scripture quoted above, how might they both act differently?
3. What could—or should—Janie do about her friends and the other kids at school who are gossiping about her?

Day 4

The Two Grandfathers

Janie was feeling even more guilty than before—she had forgotten her grandfather and his illness. She realized that she had been so busy worrying about her friends and the things she and they were doing wrong that she had neglected "Pa-pa," as she always had called her grandfather. Desperate to talk to someone and worried about Pa-pa, she finally asked her parents if she could go to the hospital and visit him.

"All right," her father suspiciously answered, "but you better not go anywhere else!"

She walked the seven blocks to the hospital with her head hung down. All the way, she wondered how long it would be before her father and mother stopped looking at her with suspicion. *After all*, she thought, *I'm not a criminal!* But a voice in her head said, "You've hurt them just the same." She ignored the voice—as she had done very frequently since she entered the sixth grade—and hurried on to the hospital.

"Yes," said the head nurse at the desk, "you can see him—but please be quiet." She pointed the way.

When Janie turned a corner, reading the room numbers, she was startled by a familiar voice. "Hi, Janie. "How're ya doin'?"

She looked toward a bench by the wall behind her; there was Chris Dobbs smiling at her. She winced, not having wanted to be seen by anyone she knew—especially Chris. "Oh—hi," she said hesitantly. "What are you doing here?"

"I came with Joshua and his grandpa to visit your grandfather," Chris explained as he stood and walked toward her. He looked closely at her. "Janie, what's wrong? Your grandfather's all right."

She tried to smile. She felt like defending herself for having treated Chris so badly—but her explanation died before she spoke. Sud-

46

denly, she blurted, "Oh, Chris, I need a friend so much!"

He reached toward her. "I'm your friend," he said, leading her to the bench. He sat beside her. "What's bugging you?"

She didn't know where to begin, and she still was cautious. She glanced at him, clasping her hands in her lap and fidgeting with them. "You're not mad at me?" she asked.

"No," he said. "I still like you a lot—though I didn't appreciate how you treated me."

Frowning, she asked, "But how *could* you still like me after—"

"Because Jesus loved and forgave the people who hurt Him—even when they were killing Him for *their* sins." Chris grinned.

She didn't know what to say. His talk about Jesus and forgiveness made her uncomfortable. But this time she did listen to the gentle voice inside herself that she had come to ignore. She moved closer to Chris. "You know, I used to believe in Jesus—and all that," she whispered. "But I think He's mad at me, too." She stiffened and began to cry.

He quickly sat up and put one arm awkwardly around her shoulders. "But Janie, Jesus isn't like your regular friends. He doesn't get mad and turn against you. That's what I learned when everyone was being mean to me because I got caught stealing."

She stared at him, wanting to believe—then hung her head. "What I did was just as bad—or worse. I lied to my parents and disobeyed them; I went to an awful movie, and now I can't forget it. And everyone in school is listening to that stupid Dotty Jensen and her gossip!" She shook her head and let it drop until her shoulder-length brown hair hung around her face. "Worst of all, I feel so *guilty.*"

"Grandpa Wiggins is the one you need to talk to," Chris decided. "Come on." He stood and led her into her grandfather's room.

Ignoring Joshua and his grandfather for the moment, Janie ran to her grandfather's bed. Crying, she laid her head on his chest. Surprised, he stroked her hair and asked, "What's the matter, little lamb?"

She looked at him with a tear-stained face and gave a weak giggle. "I feel so silly. I came to see if *you* were all right, and now you're asking *me* what's wrong." She sat up on the edge of the bed and wiped her face. Briefly, she told him everything that had happened.

He gave Grandpa Wiggins a knowing look and shook his head. "Old Satan never gives up, does he?" he asked quietly.

Janie looked from Pa-pa to Mr. Wiggins. "It was my fault," she said. "I *knew* I shouldn't go to that movie. I knew I should have listened to that voice that always speaks first and says what's right.

But. . ." She looked sadly at her grandfather.

"That quiet voice that tells you what's right," Mr. Wiggins said calmly, "is the Holy Spirit. It's *His* voice we often argue with when we want our own way rather than God's way." He smiled when Janie looked at him. "I'm not sure your parents would agree with me right now, but Janie, I'm proud of you."

"Me, too," Pa-pa agreed, hugging her against him.

She looked at both of them in disbelief. "But—why?" she asked.

"Because you're *here*," Mr. Wiggins said. "And you're not busy explaining why what you did was right. You're not blaming it on anyone else either, the way a lot of people do. And most importantly," he added, "you haven't become bitter. Bitterness is a poison people get when they walk away from God; they let Satan tempt and make them afraid, then blame God for what they got caught doing wrong. And bitterness is *awfully* hard to get rid of."

"Look after each other so that not one of you will fail to find God's best blessings. Watch out that no bitterness takes root among you, for as it springs up it causes deep trouble, hurting many in their spiritual lives" (Heb. 12:15).

Discussion Questions:
1. What good decision did Janie make in this chapter? What helped her make that decision?
2. In what ways does bitterness hurt us? How can bitterness be avoided?
3. How do you think Janie's life will be different from now on? Who or what has made it possible for her life to be different? Are her problems over?

The Fear Taker

"But I'm still in trouble," Janie protested quietly, "and I still feel guilty about what I did." She looked at Mr. Wiggins, and a frightened look came into her eyes. "Besides, I can't forget that movie! It—it's haunting me." She shuddered, and her grandfather hugged her.

Mr. Wiggins stood slowly and walked to a window. Looking out, he said, "Trouble always takes longer to get out of than it does to get into. And guilt is something that prods us in the right direction." He turned suddenly and looked straight at her eyes. "But remember, if you tell your sins to God and ask for forgiveness, He *will* forgive you."

He looked back out the window and continued, "As for your fear, just remember that the Lord Jesus Christ is a whole lot stronger than Satan. Jesus is the greatest 'Fear Taker' who's ever been or ever will be! He even told us not to be afraid—because He knew that Satan's greatest weapons are fear, guilt, and bitterness."

He sat on the foot of her grandfather's bed. His white hair almost shone, and his blue eyes were misty as he resumed. "The reason Jesus said not to be afraid is that whatever we're afraid of will come true. It will come true either in our real life or in our dreams. And Satan—in books, movies, gossip, and lots of other places—makes sure we get lots of chances to soak up his fear.

"But God wants us to wish for good things. He wants good things to come true for us. And He promised to be with us always, to comfort us like a father—even when we're tested by sickness—or gossip.

"We aren't strong, though some people like to think they are. But God *is* strong. He's stronger than fear or temptation. And He willingly offers us *His* strength. The only thing we have to do is keep ourselves turned toward him and do as He tells us. It's our choice."

Janie sighed, relaxing in her grandfather's embrace. "But what can I do about the memories of that movie? And about the gossip?"

"The Word of God," Mr. Wiggins said with a twinkle in his eyes, "is a great soap. Reading enough of the Word—the Bible—will clean anything out of us. As for me," he chuckled, looking at Mr. Warren, "I have to read it about two hours each night."

"You?" Janie asked, surprised. "But you're a good person!"

Both old men laughed, and Mr. Wiggins glanced at Joshua and Chris. "The boys'll tell you—all of us get worried, get afraid, and we get doubts. But God speaks to us through His Word; He teaches us through it. And He cleans us out with it so His Spirit can live in us."

Janie silently thought about what had been said, then leaned toward her grandfather and said, "Pa-pa, I've got to go home. I've got to get things straightened out with Mom and Daddy."

"Before you go," Mr. Wiggins said, "would you like to pray with us? We were praying when you came, and now we have two things to praise God for: your grandfather's recovery, and yours." He smiled, and they began.

On the way home, Janie frowned as she tried hard to think of ways to make her parents stop being mad at her. She tried to figure out ways to clean away her guilt and to stop being afraid. But the more she thought, the more confused and frustrated she became.

Then she heard the small, quiet voice: "*Please, Janie, lift it up to Jesus, the Fear Taker. Let Him have you and all that's yours—especially your guilts and fears.*" With a sob, she did.

She felt like ten tons of weight had been suddenly lifted off her. Her head came up; her steps lightened. Suddenly, she saw the world around her and heard birds singing. It was a different world from the gloomy, thorny one in which she'd been walking. She could hardly wait to get home!

"Mom! Daddy!" she cried as she skipped into her house. She found them in the den, recovering from the strain of Saturday lawn chores. She immediately saw that it was not the best time to be talking about problems—but she knew that the quiet voice she was hearing would guide her.

"What is it, Janie?" her father asked, barely lifting his head from the arm of the couch.

She ran to him eagerly. "I know what to say the next time some so-called friends try to get me to do something I know isn't right!"

Her father slowly sat upright. "What?" he asked quietly.

"I'll say, first, that I can't disobey my parents," Janie replied, feeling herself smiling and crying at the same time. "And second, I'll say that I belong to Jesus, who loves me like my parents do and would be hurt if I did anything that isn't what *He'd* do."

Tearfully, her mother came and wrapped her in her arms. But her father looked slightly skeptical. "That doesn't get you out of being grounded, though," he said firmly.

She knelt before him and laid both hands on his knees. "Daddy, if you treated me like Denise's parents do and didn't care what I did or didn't do, I'd think you didn't love me." She looked at him as he slowly smiled and nodded. Then she added. "Just *please* forgive me for disobeying and lying to you. I can't stand thinking that you're mad at me or don't trust me anymore."

He quickly leaned forward and hugged her with his head against hers. With a quiver in his voice that she seldom heard, he said, "Oh, honey, we forgive you." He held her for a moment, then leaned back, looked at his wife, then looked at Janie. She saw tears in his eyes, and they made her cry so hard that she almost didn't hear him say, "But we need for you to forgive us, too—for working harder than we have to, for not *being* with you enough—and," he glanced at his wife, "for not loving you the way we should."

"I forgive you," she whispered, laying her head against his knees once more. In her heart, she prayed, "*Thank you, Lord Jesus. Please teach us what it means to be a family.*" As Janie's mother joined her husband and daughter in a close embrace, peacefulness settled around them.

"*Don't worry about anything; instead, pray about everything; tell God your needs and don't forget to thank him for his answers. If you do this you will experience God's peace...*" (Phil. 4:6-7a).

Discussion Questions:
1. Read Romans 8:28. How did God use Janie's bad experiences to her, and her parents', benefit?
2. Read 1 Corinthians 10:13. Is there *any* problem we cannot take to the Lord?
3. What do you think Janie should do about Denise Kibler? List at least five things Janie and her parents could do from now on to become the family Jesus wants them to be.

The Quiet Voice

Day 1

Gossip!

The girls on the school playground were talking, and Janie was listening.

"Did'ja hear about Denise Kibler?"

"I heard her parents split up."

"I heard her father beat her up. Did'ja see her right eye?"

"Yeah, it's all black."

"Serves her right! Who's she think she is anyhow? Just 'cause she had that gang of Fraidy Cats for a while made her think she was hot stuff!"

"And she was sent to the principal's office twice last week—once for fighting, once for talking back to the teacher. I heard that if she gets sent down there one more time, she'll be expelled."

"Serves her right!"

"Shhh! Here she comes!"

The girls drifted apart, glancing sideways at Denise, who was coming toward them with a sullen look—and a black eye. Janie lowered her gaze so she wouldn't have to look at Denise, and slowly she walked toward the large group of kids playing soccer. Chris Dobbs and Joshua Wiggins were standing on the sideline, waiting for a turn to play. She stopped beside them.

Chris glanced at her, then looked again. "What's wrong?" he asked quietly. "Did somebody hurt you?"

"No, nothing's wrong," Janie said, keeping her eyes toward the ground.

"Do you want to talk about it later?" Chris whispered so the other kids wouldn't hear. After all, Janie had taken enough teasing for going to church with Joshua and him; he didn't want to cause her more embarrassment by being seen talking to her on the playground!

After school, Joshua and Chris went to Janie's house. She led them into the backyard so they could talk in private, sitting around the trunk of the oak tree. Janie told the boys what the gossips were saying about Denise. Then she said, "And I sort of agree with them; it *does* serve Denise right! She got me—and several other people—in trouble. She gossips about everybody she hears the least bit of dirt about—and she thinks she's tough. We'll just see how tough she is now!" She looked at Chris and Joshua who were picking at the dirt with twigs.

The boys glanced at each other, but they said nothing. Their expressions were sad and puzzled.

"Okay," Janie sighed, "let's have it; let's hear your advice."

But still the boys said nothing.

Impatiently, Janie stood and went to the swing. She sat and began kicking her feet, making the swing jerk to one side, then the other. "Aren't you going to tell me that as a Christian, I should try to help Denise instead of being like the other kids?" Neither Josh nor Chris answered her. "Aren't you going to tell me that Denise needs Jesus and that now would be a good time to try to talk to her about becoming a Christian?" When the boys still did not answer her, she hung her head and began swinging straight back and forth.

Sheepishly, she said, "I guess I should talk to her." She raised her head and looked at the boys as she let the swing coast to a stop. "After all, isn't that what I'm supposed to do—for her sake—and mine?"

"And so I am giving a new commandment to you now—love each other just as much as I love you. Your strong love for each other will prove to the world that you are my disciples" (John 13:34-35).

Discussion Questions:

1. How does Janie feel about Denise? At this point, do you think Janie really understands what the Lord means in the scriptures quoted above—about loving one another as much as He loved us?

2. Why do you suppose there often is such conflict between what *we* naturally want to do about something or someone and what *God* wants us to do? (See Isaiah 55:8 and Romans 7:18.) What, then, is Janie's "battle"?

3. How would you approach Denise Kibler with the message of salvation?

Day 2

Rejection

Janie Warren worked up her courage and met Denise the next morning on the way to school. Denise walked right past her, and Janie hurried to keep up. Janie was trembling inside, but she felt sure she was doing the right thing. Besides, she could tell just by looking at Denise that she was in pain; Denise's face was puffy, as though she had been crying, and she was frowning tightly.

"I'd still like to be your friend," Janie began. Her words rushed out, and she hardly could believe she'd said them.

Denise didn't answer. Instead, she walked on—head down, her arms wrapped around her school books.

Janie took a deep breath, thinking that since she'd managed to begin, at least she could go on and finish. "I think you need to meet a friend of mine who's helped me a lot—Jesus Christ."

Denise's head snapped around, and she gave Janie a sneering look. "Don't start on me with that religious stuff!"

"But you need help," Janie persisted. "And—"

"Shut up!" Denise snapped, stopping on the sidewalk and giving Janie a warning look. "You listen to me, Miss Goody-goody! I don't care what you think—and I don't care what you think I need! What's more, you're not my friend and you never were. I just let you in the Fraidy Cats 'cause you kept hanging around us." With a jerk she resumed walking down the sidewalk. Janie stood and watched her, feeling as though she had been in a fistfight.

Janie went through the rest of the day with the miserable feeling that she had *failed.* She couldn't believe even Denise had been so mean to her—though inside she really had expected just that kind of treatment. Still, she was embarrassed, and she heard herself think, "Boy, it'll be a *long* time before I *ever* stick my neck out like *that* again!"

As she was walking home from school, the last two people in the world she wanted to see right then caught up with her: Joshua and

Chris. They walked beside her, one on each side, even though she wouldn't look at them.

"Well," Chris began, "how'd it go with Denise?"

"How do you *think* it went?" Janie snapped, feeling mad at Chris—as though he had talked her into making a fool of herself.

"There's a place in the Bible," Joshua quietly said, "where Jesus told His disciples, *'Don't worry about what to say at your trial, for you will be given the right words at the right time. For it won't be you doing the talking—'* "*

"You memorized that?" Janie asked, coming to a stop.

"Sure," Joshua said, blinking. "If I didn't memorize verses from the Bible, it would be *me* talking when I tell other people about Jesus."

Janie walked on, shaking her head. "I sure wasn't given the right words, then, 'cause Denise didn't even listen."

"Did you ask the Holy Spirit to help you?" Josh asked.

"No," Janie said hesitantly. "I guess I was too busy just trying not to hate Denise for what she did."

They walked on for a while before Joshua said, "If you really want to help Denise, you'll have to love her, you know."

Janie looked at him as though he'd just told her she would have to eat nothing but spinach for a month.

Josh laughed. "Sorry, but Grandpa says that's the only way things work. And he says that when Jesus told us to love our enemies and pray for those who persecute us, He didn't mean we should feel some kind of mushy-gushy love for them. We can't. Grandpa says that what Jesus meant was that we have to *choose* to love people like Denise the way God loves them. We have to show them *God's* love, which means putting aside our own feelings and seeing people the way God sees them."

Janie felt as if she was being asked to leap off a high cliff. "Chris. . . ?" she began, turning to him. He grinned and shyly took her hand. As Joshua turned the corner to go home, Chris and Janie walked on—holding hands and talking quietly.

"He told his disciples, 'I have been given all authority (power) in heaven and earth. Therefore go and make disciples in all the nations. . .'" (Matt. 28:18-19a).

---

*Matthew 10:19, 20

Discussion Questions:

1. What were the results of Janie's talk with Denise? Would you have any suggestions for her?
2. Why would Jesus tell His disciples: "I have been given all power... *Therefore*, go..."? Or, to ask the question differently, how did eleven ordinary, frightened (see John 20:19) men from a small country in a corner of the Roman Empire manage to conquer the world for Jesus? What power was available to them that also is available to us?
3. In what ways is God's love different from the love we usually feel?

Day 3

The Punishment

Several weeks went by—weeks of study and thinking for Janie Warren. For Denise Kibler, however, they were weeks of misery. Janie and the other kids heard from their parents that Denise's parents had, in fact, separated. Denise was living with her mother, and her father had taken an apartment on the other side of town. When Janie heard that news, she began to pray that she would be given another chance to help Denise find the way out of her pain.

For her part, Denise simply became tougher and tougher, and more and more sullen. Then, one Friday, matters came to a head. It happened on the playground. Lori Matthews was running after one of the other girls in a game of keep-away when she bumped into Denise. Denise whirled around and shoved Lori as hard as she could. Lori fell backward, hitting the back of her head on one of the jungle gym bars.

"Oh, she's *bleeding*!" one of the girls cried, watching Lori sit up and put one hand to the back of her head.

Kids swarmed around, trying to see, and some yelled, "Here comes Mrs. Simmons!"

The P.E. teacher worked her way into the center of the crowd and examined Lori's wound. Another teacher came, and Mrs. Simmons said, "Take Lori to the nurse and call her mother. I think she'll have to have stitches." She watched as the other teacher led Lori, who was stumbling and crying, toward the school building.

The kids, meanwhile, were buzzing. "Wow, stitches!" "Did you see the *blood*?" "Did'ja see the way she just *pushed* her?"

"Who pushed her?" Mrs. Simmons demanded, turning to look at the children around her.

They fell silent. Looking at one another, they tensely waited for someone to break the silence.

"I said, *who did it*!" Mrs. Simmons demanded, more loudly, fists on her waist.

One by one, several of the kids began glancing at Denise. Even though no one liked her anymore, no one was going to tell. But they did turn slightly and look at her. Mrs. Simmons looked too. "Well?"

The kids around Denise moved out of the way as though they thought lightning was about to strike. Denise shot them angry looks—and saw Janie watching her. "She did it!" Denise shouted, stabbing one finger toward Janie. "She shoved her down, and I saw her!"

Several of the kids muttered, but no one said anything. Mrs. Simmons turned toward Janie. "Well?" she asked. "Did you?"

Janie felt frozen, petrified. In that instant, she heard a quiet voice inside her head say, "One more time, and she'll be expelled." Looking at Mrs. Simmons, Janie neither denied nor confirmed the accusation.

Mrs. Simmons took Janie straight to the principal's office. Her parents were called, and when her mother came to the school, it was decided that her punishment for injuring another student was that she would have to stay thirty minutes after school each day for two weeks—and be put on probation. During the conference, Janie kept her head down. She could feel her mother, the principal, and Mrs. Simmons staring at her. She felt urges to cry, to explain, to deny—but the quiet voice in her head kept assuring her, "It'll be all right—just wait."

"If you refuse to take up your cross and follow me, you are not worthy of being mine. If you cling to your life, you will lose it; but if you give it up for me, you will save it'" (Matt. 10:38-39).

Discussion Questions:
1. Was Janie's punishment fair? Why do you suppose the quiet voice inside her prompted her to be silent and take the punishment?
2. What did Jesus mean by asking us to give up our lives for Him? How can we give something up, yet save it?
3. Is being a Christian an easy thing to do? What kinds of help do we have?

Day 4

Why?

Janie didn't see Denise Kibler much the next week; Denise seemed to be avoiding everybody. But harder than the possibility of seeing Denise was having to deal with the other kids. They said all sorts of things to her.

"Boy, I'd have told who did it! What'd you keep your mouth shut for?"

"Who cares about Denise, anyhow? As mean as she is, I hope they do kick her out of school!"

It was all Janie could do to keep from answering.

Finally, Friday came—the last day of the first week of Janie's punishment. After school, as she was walking home, Denise confronted her. They were halfway between school and Janie's home when Denise stepped out from behind a tree. Janie stopped and watched her, trying to put the love she knew God felt for Denise into her own expression. She felt herself smiling as tears came into her eyes.

Denise stopped about a yard in front of her, silently studying Janie's expression. Then she said, "Why? Why'd you take what was coming to me?" When Janie didn't reply, Denise shook her head with a half-sneer and said, "That was the *dumbest* thing I've ever seen anybody do!"

Janie grinned, wiping her eyes, and nodded. "I guess so," she managed to say.

Denise looked away, nibbling at the insides of her lips. "But why'd you do it?" she asked quietly.

"'Cause God loves you."

Denise glared at Janie. Her expression was hard, unbelieving—but tears crept into her eyes. Suddenly she screamed, "Liar!" Backing away, she screamed again, "Liar! He doesn't love me! He's not even real!" She turned and ran up the sidewalk as fast as she could, her stringy blond hair flying behind her.

" 'Look! I have been standing at the door and I am constantly knocking. If anyone hears me calling him and opens the door, I will come in and fellowship with him and he with me' " (Rev. 3:20).

" 'Those who welcome you are welcoming me. And when they welcome me they are welcoming God who sent me' " (Matt. 10:40).

Discussion Questions:

1. How did Denise treat Janie? How could Janie—having learned all that she has learned—not be mad at Denise or be hurt by her? Who is Denise actually rejecting?

2. When Jesus said, "...and opens the door," what "door" is He talking about? In what way will He come in? What does "fellowship with him and he with me" mean?

3. Why do you think Denise is being so tough? What do you think Janie should do now? (See Ephesians 6:18.)

Day 5

"You're Different"

By the end of the second week of Janie Warren's punishment, the general opinion among the kids in the sixth grade was that she was a real dummy. For that reason, Joshua and Chris made sure they were waiting outside the school when Janie finally could leave. Each day they walked her home—usually without saying much. They didn't say much because all three of them were waiting for something to happen—something they and their parents had been praying for.

That Friday, the end of the second week, Janie, Josh, and Chris were almost to her home when once again Denise stepped out from behind a tree. The two boys looked at each other and at Janie, then left without saying anything. Denise slowly walked up to Janie.

"Well?" she asked sarcastically. "Don't you want to know what I want?"

Janie smiled. "I'm glad to see you no matter what you want."

"Don't be corny!" Denise snapped. "I know you hate me. Everybody does!" She looked closely at Janie to watch her reaction.

There were many things Janie knew she could say—arguments, explanations, denials. Instead of speaking, however, she concentrated on trying to see Denise the way she knew Jesus saw her. And, strangely, she saw a terribly frightened, hurt, lonely girl. She wanted very much to hug her, to brush her stringy hair and make it beautiful as she saw it could be—but she knew Denise would just push her away and laugh at her.

"What's wrong with you?" Denise demanded uncomfortably, seeing Janie's expression—and tears.

"I just love you, that's all."

Denise stiffened, became more uncomfortable, and hung her head. "I don't deserve your love—or anybody else's."

Janie cautiously approached her and put one arm around her shoulders. She felt Denise tremble, start to pull away, then slowly relax.

"You—you're *different*," Denise muttered as they began walking up the sidewalk toward Janie's house. "You're different from the other kids—and you're different from the way I thought you were." She wiped her eyes, then looked at Janie sideways, shyly. "How come?"

Janie took a deep breath, smiling. "Because Jesus loves me—like He loves you."

A flicker of disbelief flashed across Denise's expression, and for a moment she frowned. But she could not deny the look in Janie's eyes nor the comforting warmth of her touch. Looking at the sidewalk, Denise mumbled, "Is that what it means to be a Christian?"

Joy flared up in Janie's heart. "Partly," she said, letting the joy flood into her expression. As Denise studied her face, Janie said, "And it also means, 'If you tell others with your own mouth that Jesus Christ is your Lord, and believe in your own heart that God has raised him from the dead, you will be saved.' "*

"Saved?" Denise asked. "What d'you mean, 'saved'? From what?"

Thanking God in her heart for answered prayers, Janie quietly said, "Can you come home with me for a while? I'd rather show you in God's Word—the Bible—than tell you in my own words."

Denise nodded, wiping her face and sniffing. "Sure, I can go home with you. Mom's working and Dad's—gone."

"Don't worry," Janie said softly. "Through Jesus, even your parents. . ." They walked on, close together, talking quietly.

From hiding places behind a row of bushes, Joshua and Chris stood up. Grinning broadly, they shook hands and ran to Joshua's house to tell his grandfather what they had seen!

"Again I say, we are telling you about what we ourselves have actually seen and heard, so that you may share the fellowship and the joys we have with the Father and with Jesus Christ his Son. And if you do as I say in this letter, then you, too, will be full of joy, and so will we" (1 John 1:3-4).

Discussion Questions:
1. What were Janie, Joshua, and Chris so happy about? How did they express their happiness? What does the following verse have to do with Denise's story: "For everything comes from God alone.

---

*Romans 10:9

Everything lives by his power, and everything is for his glory. To him be glory evermore" (Rom. 11:36)?

2. Does anyone you know think of Christianity as being a solemn, "thou-shalt-not," fear-filled religion? What would the Apostle John—judging from John 1:3-4—say to such people? What might Janie, Chris, Joshua, or—later—Denise say to such people?

3. What do you think will happen next to Denise—and to her parents?

WEEK FIVE
Called Together

Day 1

"No!"

"No!" shouted Denise Kibler's mother. "I don't *want* him back! He beat *me* up, he beat *you* up, and it was *his* decision to move out!"

Denise looked sadly at the Christmas tree she and her mother were decorating. "But, Mom, *you* said you didn't want him any more—you told him to—"

"And I'm telling you, I don't want to hear any more about it! The divorce has been filed. In twenty-nine more days, we'll have a hearing. And then. . . " She sobbed once and slumped, dropping the shiny red ball she had been about to hang.

Denise quickly laid one hand on her mother's back and stroked her. "See, Mom, you want him back as much as I do, but — "

"But nothing!" she snapped. Her mother stiffened, throwing off Denise's hand. She held her head up proudly and tightened her lower jaw. In a softer, more dejected voice she added, "I'm tired of having to work all day, come home and cook, clean *and* fight with him! My life is just plain simpler without him!" She set her jaw again and began hanging the bright red balls on the sweet-smelling fir limbs.

Without another word, Denise stood and began to leave the room.

"Where're you going?" her mother asked, giving her an almost frightened look. Since her husband had left, she frequently was afraid, and several times she had awakened Denise in the middle of the night—crying and crying, then going silently back to her bed.

"I was going to see Janie. May I?"

"Couldn't we finish trimming the tree first?" her mother asked, almost pleading.

Denise grinned. "Sure," she said, coming back to help her mother.

" 'Do you permit divorce?' they asked."

" 'Don't you read the Scriptures?' he replied. 'In them it is written that at the beginning God created man and woman, and that a man should leave his father and mother, and be forever united to his wife. The two shall become one—no longer two, but one! And no man may divorce what God has joined together' " (Matt. 19:3c-6).

Discussion Questions:
1. What does Denise want? What do you think her mother wants?
2. Which do you think the Kiblers are thinking more of: themselves and their own "rights" OR the desires and commands of Jesus Christ? How could one ("rights") get in the way of the other (Jesus)?
3. If you were Denise, what would you do next?

Day 2

Be Subject

When Denise went to visit Janie, Janie suggested they both talk with Grandpa Wiggins. Sitting before a crackling fire in the Wiggins' fireplace later that afternoon, he listened patiently. When Denise had finished telling about her parent's situation, he reached to the mantel and took down a Bible.

"Ephesians 5:21 through 25 has the answer," he said, then began to read: "Honor Christ by submitting to each other. You wives must submit to your husbands' leadership in the same way you submit to the Lord. For a husband is in charge of his wife in the same way Christ is in charge of his body the church. (He gave his very life to take care of it and be its Savior!) So you wives must willingly obey your husbands in everything, just as the church obeys Christ. And you husbands, show the same kind of love to your wives as Christ showed to the church when he died for her. ...." He also read Matthew 19:3-6 (which you read yesterday), then said, "Christ was pretty clear about how important marriage—and a family—is to him. Marriage between a husband and a wife is just like the marriage between Christ and his church. If the relationship is broken...." He spread his hands and gave the girls a sad look.

"But how do I get them to listen?" Denise asked, wanting a simple, quick answer that she could use to make everything all right again—now.

Grandpa Wiggins closed the Bible and laid it back on the mantel. "What got *you* to begin listening?" he asked.

Denise glanced at Janie with a shy smile. "Love did—God's love through my friend there."

"Well, there's your solution," Grandpa Wiggins said softly.

Denise frowned, rubbing her hands together and looking at them. "But Mom's still *mad*—and Dad's living on the other side of town."

"Do you need a ride?" Grandpa asked.

"No—I mean, not yet," Denise said, flustered. She nibbled the insides of her lips, frowning as she thought about trying to talk to her father—whom she hadn't seen in two weeks.

"When you go," Grandpa advised, "be sure you take your Bible. Do you understand what it means by 'submitting'?"

"I think so," Denise said hesitantly. "It means giving in."

"Ah, but much more than that," Grandpa said. "If you tell me what to do, and I just give in to you, then later I'm probably going to resent you, and maybe I'll even get madder at you than before I gave in."

"Then what...?"

He gazed into the warm fire. "The Bible says to submit to *each other*—both at the same time—in the same way we submit to Jesus Christ. That means putting Christ first."

"So my parents've got to give their hearts to Jesus first?"

"And let Him have all their 'rights.' If we're truly His servants, we have no rights of our own."

"Oh, my," Denise groaned. "Getting my parents to see that would be like—like convincing King Kong to wash dishes without breaking them."

Grandpa laughed, then hugged Denise to him. "But, honey, *you* don't have to do the work. You're a servant yourself, and your *Master* has all the power, all the words, and all the love necessary."

"But what if it doesn't work out? What if they don't—?"

He hugged her again. "Do you want what *you* want, or what God wants? I mean, are you worried that you may not be satisfied or that God may not be?"

Denise hung her head in thought, then looked shyly at Grandpa Wiggins. "You mean, it could be God's will that they not get back together?"

"I mean, all you can do is keep obeying Jesus and praying that God will give you power to do what *He* wants done. Only if you do that will your parents see that more is involved than just what you or they want."

She kissed his cheek. "I love you, Grandpa Wiggins," she said, " 'cause I can see Jesus in you."

"And I love you, too—for the same reason," he said gently.

"Dear brothers, if a Christian is overcome by some sin, you who are godly should gently and humbly help him back onto the right path, remembering that next time it might be one of you who is in the wrong" (Gal. 6:1).

70

Discussion Questions:

1. Tell about at least one thing Denise learned from Grandpa Wiggins.
2. What is risky or difficult about trying to help others—especially friends who are having trouble? Have you ever been told, "Mind your own business!"? How does Paul's advice to the Galatians help?
3. What more can Grandpa Wiggins and Janie do to help Denise? What can Denise do before she goes to see her father and talks to her mother again?

Day 3

The Plea

"Please, Mom," Denise said, sitting close in front of her on the carpet, "it's only three days 'til Christmas Eve. Will you at least go with me to church then—and not say no if Dad says he wants to talk with you?"

Her mother sighed and unfolded her arms as she watched the lights flashing on the Christmas tree. "I haven't been to church since I was eleven," she said quietly, "when my mother took me to that revival meeting."

"When you asked Jesus into your heart?"

"Yes," her mother murmured, looking down at Denise. "I haven't exactly been following Him, have I?" She smiled briefly. "And I won't say no—provided your father is *serious* this time about working things out."

"Thanks, Mom!" Denise said, jumping up to get her Bible.

"Where're you going?"

"To talk to Dad."

"Now?" When Denise nodded vigorously, her mother sighed and started to get up. "Well, at least let me take you over there."

"No, thanks. I want to walk," Denise said, putting on her coat and gloves. She smiled at her mother. "I want to talk with God as I go."

It took her thirty minutes to walk to her father's apartment—and about five to work up the courage to knock. When she finally did, her heart was beating with big thumps. To Denise's relief, her father quickly opened the door. He seemed surprised to see her, and he hesitated before inviting her in. She sat on the couch while he poured her a soft drink, then sat at the opposite end of the couch, picking lint from his pants.

"What brings you out in this cold weather?" he asked, making an effort to smile at her.

She wondered why he seemed so anxious—and formal—with her,

72

but she told him why she had come. As she talked about marriage and the Bible, his anxiousness increased until he abruptly stood and paced to the other side of the small living room. Denise swirled the ice cubes around in her glass and finished by saying, "So, if you divorce Mom, it'll just be wrong all the way around—for you and her, for me—and for God."

He laughed, plopping down in a chair. "Don't be silly, Denise. I love you, but your mother and I just do not get along! God knows I tried to put up with her—always worrying about the bills, about where I was when I had to work late, about—"

"Please, Dad," Denise interrupted quietly. "I know what the fights were about. But getting a divorce is worse than all the screaming and fighting and slamming doors. And if either of you tried to get remarried that would be—"

"Oh, don't be silly! Half the people in this country have gotten divorces. There're just so many pressures on people, so many—problems. Besides, if we do get divorced, you'll still see me."

"Yes, but I won't have a father when I need one!" she cried, setting down her glass and running to kneel at his feet. "And I love you; I miss you, and I *know* Mom misses you."

He looked away with a disgruntled expression. "Fat chance," he muttered.

"She does, and she's willing to try to work things out—if you are."

He stood quickly and walked away from her, saying, "Work things out? She won't even listen to me! And she's got you convinced that everything's *my* fault!" He glared at Denise, who slowly stood. "I never saw so much *nerve*—sending a child to do her dirty work!"

"Dad!" Denise cried, hurt and confused. "It was my idea to—"

"Well, you just get on home," he stormed, "and tell your mother her little trick failed. I don't need her and her problems," he added, turning on Denise. "And I don't need you—or anybody else! So, get out!"

Crying, stunned because things had gone all wrong, Denise left. Her father slammed the door behind her, and she had a long, cold walk home.

"O my rebellious children, come back to me again and I will heal you from your sins. And they reply, Yes, we will come, for you are the Lord our God" (Jer. 3:22).

" 'Then who in the world can be saved?' they asked. Jesus looked at them intently and said, 'Humanly speaking, no one. But with God, everything is possible' " (Matt. 19:25b-26).

" 'Happy are those who strive for peace—they shall be called the sons of God' " (Matt. 5:9).

Discussion Questions:
1. How did Mr. Kibler respond to Denise's plea? Why do you think he was so bitter?
2. What can Denise do now?
3. Even though Denise is sad and hurt, in what way could she also be happy—and find comfort?

Day 4

The Cry

The next morning Denise didn't even want to get out of bed. She cried until she was tired of crying. Then she became mad—mad at her father, mad at her mother. She thumped her pillow with both fists, wishing she had somebody to fight or beat up; at least when she fought with her fists, she got rid of the frustration she felt inside herself. Finally, she wore herself out. It was then that her eyes strayed to the Bible Janie Warren had given her. She picked it up and thumbed through it. Her eyes lighted on Jesus' Sermon on the Mount, and she read the words, "Happy are those who strive for peace. . . ."

"Happy!" she thought sadly. "A lot of good it did me! All that happened was that I wound up being a *target.*" She sighed and started to close the Bible—but she didn't. As her hand rested on it, a small, quiet voice inside her said, "Yes, happy—because you did what God wanted you to. If your father—or you—keeps being angry, he—like you—will keep being in pain." She instantly remembered how happy she had been when Janie and Janie's mother had shown her how she could get rid of the pain she had felt inside.

"Oh, Dad," she murmured, "I want you to quit hurting, too!" She prayed; then she set out again for her father's apartment.

He was not too happy to see her. He let her in with a suspicious look, and he remained standing with his arms folded as she sat on a chair.

When she didn't say anything—and just looked at him with tears in her eyes—he became impatient. "Well?" he asked, huffing as he walked toward the kitchen. "What do you want today?" He leaned on the bar between the kitchen and living room and skeptically watched her.

Taking off her gloves and clasping her sweating hands, she said, "Dad, tomorrow night's Christmas Eve. The church I've been going to is having a special service. I—I'm going to make a public testimony of faith—faith in Jesus Christ. I want you to be there."

He straightened and came into the living room. Denise couldn't tell if his expression was one of anger or puzzlement. "Why would you want to do that?" he asked.

She felt her tension and anxiety flow out of her, and she smiled at her father as though nothing bad ever had happened between them. "Because I love Jesus," she said softly. "I love Him for loving me, for picking me up and taking away my pain and—and loneliness, and for leading me to friends who love me for what I am—not for how tough I am."

He shook his head and sat on the couch with a sigh. Rubbing his eyes, he took a deep breath and let it out. Looking at her again, he said, "I'm glad for you. I wish I could feel something when I go to church. But it's been twenty years."

"Dad, it's not what I *feel*," Denise said gently. "It's what I *know*, what I've *seen*—things that I wouldn't have believed were possible either—until I stopped saying 'No!' to God and started listening."

He raised one eyebrow and half-smiled at her. "Are you saying I haven't been listening, that I—"

"No, sir," she said. "I'm just saying why I'm going to tell about my commitment tomorrow night, and why I want you to be there more than anything else I've ever wanted. Dad, I love you. *I love you!*"

"I—I don't know," he muttered looking away. Abruptly, he stood and paced toward the kitchen. "Some of the people where I work are having a party tomorrow night. I told them I'd come—so I don't know." He glanced at her, and they were silent for a while.

At last, Denise nodded and began putting her gloves back on.

"I'll think about it," he said lamely, walking with her to the door. She turned, stretched up, and kissed his cheek. Then she left. He stood in the doorway watching her go up the street, shivered, and closed the door, shaking his head with a troubled look.

"But the wisdom that comes from heaven is first of all pure and full of quiet gentleness. Then it is peace-loving and courteous. It allows discussion and is willing to yield to others; it is full of mercy and good deeds. It is wholehearted and straightforward and sincere. And those who are peacemakers will plant seeds of peace and reap a harvest of goodness" (James 3:17-18).

Discussion Questions:
1. What did Denise do or say differently the second time she visited her father? What can she do if things still don't work out?
2. What is Mr. Kibler's basic choice?
3. At the moment, what is Denise's biggest "test"?

Day 5

Called Together

The next day, Denise surprised herself; as she waited to go to the church service that night, she was calm. Her mother, on the other hand, was as jumpy as a bird being stalked by three cats. When Janie Warren and her parents came by with a fruitcake, Mrs. Kibler practically ran to answer the doorbell; she talked excitedly and was extremely glad to see the Warrens, to have visitors, and to be given the cake. But when they left, she again became edgy—then again went through the whole jump-and-run routine when Joshua Wiggins and his grandfather came with a present for her and one for Denise. By the time Chris Dobbs stopped to leave a present for Denise, Mrs. Kibler was worn out.

Therefore, when they finally went to the church, Mrs. Kibler was fairly relaxed. She kept her eyes lowered—afraid of the looks people who knew she hadn't been to church in a *long* time would be giving her. She seemed embarrassed when the Warrens, Matthews, and finally the Wiggins stopped at her pew to say how glad they were to see her and Denise. And by then, it was Denise's turn to be nervous. Frequently, she turned to look toward the back of the church—hoping . . . praying . . . hoping.

The service began as a thanksgiving to God for sending His Son. The congregation—which filled the church—sang two songs, then a third as Denise continued to look around the end of the pew and up the aisle. He wasn't there. Denise clenched her lips as she used to do before going into a fight. With the same kind of courage and determination, she thought, "I'm not going to give up! I'm *not* going to stop praying! I'm *not!*"

The pastor took his place behind the pulpit and began his sermon. Denise forced herself to listen as he began telling how God, the Father of Light and the source of all goodness, long had desired and planned to bring His children out of darkness and back to himself. When he began telling how Christ had come to open a way for God's children to come back to Him, Denise heard a low whisper—"Scoot over."

With surprised delight, Denise moved over to let her father sit beside her. He grinned sideways at her, but he avoided looking at her mother or at the people around them. He seemed terribly embarrassed—or afraid—to be where he was, doing what he was.

Denise decided to do something quickly before he could leave. She took his left hand in both her hands and squeezed it. She heard him let out the breath he'd been holding and almost laugh. Immediately, she reached and took her mother's right hand, placed it in her lap—despite her mother's mild struggle to resist—and plopped her father's hand on top. Covering both their hands with her own hands, Denise sighed, smiling contentedly, and began listening to the pastor again.

She could feel her parents' hands under hers almost twitching, itching, hesitant, about to jerk away any instant. But she kept both in place, covered by her own hands, and gradually they began to grow warm and relax. Denise grinned at each of them, ignoring the people nearby who were glancing their way. The pastor, meanwhile, was telling about the purpose for the coming of Jesus Christ—how it was the fulfillment of centuries of prophecies and the climax of God's great plan. He told about the plan for the salvation of mankind, and he told how Jesus made that plan possible with His death. Then, he came down from the podium and stood at the altar.

He began, "If there are those here who would like to publicly show that they have received Jesus and died with Christ to sin..." Denise felt something swelling up within her. She was almost afraid, but the sensation was too powerful to resist. Before she knew it, she was on her feet, working her way past her father, and going—almost running—down the aisle to the altar. There, she knelt, seeing neither the people around nor the pastor, but seeing only Christ's light calling her into life.

It seemed like a long, long time before she heard one of the deacons saying, "What's your name, child? Are these your parents?"

Denise looked through her tears—and saw her mother standing nearby. Her father, looking scared and happy at the same time, was standing beside her mother. "Yes!" Denise cried happily. "They're my parents!"

"Jesus said to the people, 'I am the Light of the world. So if you follow me, you won't be stumbling through the darkness, for living light will flood your path'" (John 8:12).

Discussion Questions:

1. Earlier in this chapter, what was Mrs. Kibler nervous about? And what was Denise anxious about? Find a Bible passage that would have helped both of them.
2. What changed Mr. and Mrs. Kibler? What might be different in their lives from now on?

WEEK SIX

Into the Wilderness

Day 1

Adventure!

"Skillet?" asked Grandpa Wiggins.

"Check," said Joshua.

"Matches?"

"Check."

"Sleeping bags and liners?"

"Check."

"I still think," began Mrs. Wiggins, "that it's not a good idea to be taking the boys camping in such cold weather."

Mr. Wiggins patiently looked at her, pushing his glasses up on his nose. "A little hardship never hurt anyone, Dorothy. Not even you."

Mrs. Wiggins watched with folded arms as Grandpa and Joshua went on checking through the mound of supplies and equipment; later with the same expression, she watched them drive off to pick up Chris Dobbs and David Matthews. "Lord, keep them warm!" she prayed.

Keeping warm proved to be a major undertaking for the boys. Snow lay four inches deep on the ground and was drifted waist-deep near the edge of the forest of the Kiameche Wilderness. The boys worked hard to clear a space in which to pitch the tent, and they worked even harder finding enough firewood to last through the night—which promised to be very cold and snowy.

"This is the life!" Grandpa declared as soon as the fire was burning well. He held his gloved hands out to the blaze and rubbed them together. His pale blue eyes sparkled above his cold-reddened cheeks as he looked at each of the boys—especially David Matthews, who was a year younger than Chris and Josh. "How're you doing?" he asked David.

The boy shrugged, glancing toward the dark shadows under the snow-draped limbs of the forest. "Okay—I guess. But when we were gathering firewood, I thought I heard a wolf howl."

"Most likely," Grandpa said cheerfully, digging a pot from the "kitchen pack." He poured milk into it so he could make hot chocolate, then said, "All kinds of animals out here—maybe even black bear."

"Bear?" Chris asked, his eyes widening. He watched Grandpa hang the pot full of milk on a green stick over the blaze. "Won't they smell our food?"

"Only if they wake up from their hibernation," Grandpa said, chuckling.

The boys huddled around the campfire, holding their hands out to the warmth—and occasionally glancing behind themselves at the vast, snow-covered wilderness. "Sure is quiet," Joshua whispered.

"Nobody for miles around," Chris added. "Not even rangers."

They fell silent for a while—and in the silence, the boys began to think about television, record players, central heating, and *warm beds*.

"What if a blizzard comes," David wondered aloud, "and we get *stuck* here?"

"We'd have to survive—and depend more than ever on the Lord," Grandpa said, "the way Christians a long time ago had to do—when there were a lot more wild animals and a lot fewer cities, police, and lights."

"Lights?" Chris asked in a small voice, looking around at the darkening gray sky. He turned up his collar against a sudden, cold gust.

"Haven't you ever been far, far away from any towns before?" Grandpa asked. "Out here, there aren't any lights—no street lights or house lights or even car lights."

As nighttime closed in, the boys huddled closer and closer to the campfire, hoping they had gathered enough wood to last the night. It seemed that the only thing between them and the dark, silent, cold wilderness was the flickering light of the campfire.

Later, when they went into the tent and snuggled inside their bedrolls, the fire died. Then, there was no light. The wolves began to howl.

"The disciples went to [Jesus] and wakened him, shouting, 'Lord,

save us! We're sinking!' But Jesus answered, 'O you men of little faith! Why are you so frightened?' Then he stood up and rebuked the wind and waves, and the storm subsided and all was calm" (Matt. 8:25-26).

Discussion Questions:
1. Of what were the boys afraid? Have you ever been afraid of things like that? What did you imagine would happen to you?
2. Of what is Jesus Christ Lord? After reading the above scripture, why do you think Jesus was sleeping while the others worried?
3. How do you think *God* feels about nature—all of nature? How do you think He wants *us* to feel about—and treat—nature?

Day 2

Up the River

The fifth member of the camping expedition was Tiff, David Matthews' dog. He had spent the night at the foot of David's sleeping bag—inside it, of course. Early, early in the morning Tiff scrambled out of the bag and wormed his way through the tied flaps of the tent door. When David managed to get dressed—shivering violently—and go outside, he saw his dog standing motionless, one forepaw raised as he sniffed of something. David went to see what Tiff was sniffing. Pushing his black hair under the edge of his parka, he bent over. "Hey, WOW!," he shouted, startling Tiff. "Come 'ere, you guys!"

As quickly as they could, Chris and Joshua joined David and looked down where he was pointing. There, pressed deeply into the snow was a line of prints—paw prints, big ones. "*Wolves!*" David breathed, watching his breath come out like a white, curling feather.

"Look, they're headed for the river," Joshua said, staring at the line of wandering tracks.

"Let's follow them," Chris suggested, starting off.

"Whoa," Grandpa called, coming out of the tent with their skillet in hand, "not before breakfast."

They rebuilt the fire from embers buried under a layer of ashes, and Grandpa soon had cooked eggs and bacon, pan toast and gravy. He put two metal buckets packed with snow on the fire while they ate and drank milk and orange juice; when the snow was melted he showed the boys how to do a good job washing dishes. When their gear was put back in its place, they set off—up the river.

When they entered the forest, the boys felt their fear of the wilderness return. All was silent under the snow-draped trees, and a cold wind whipped along the drifts and raised sparkling crystal whiskers. A squirrel stepped from its leaf-ball nest high in a bare, white-skinned sycamore tree and chattered angrily down at the boys, twitching its bushy tail. Tiff barked back at the squirrel, but David made him follow so he wouldn't get lost. Teeth chattering, David asked, "What if one of us got lost out here? What if—?"

"Sorry," Grandpa interrupted, "but you can't play the 'what if' game in the wilderness. If you do, you miss seeing 'what *is*.'"

And the first "what *is*" they came to was a great deadfall of tangled tree trunks, branches, and drifted snow. A hole went into the deadfall—a dark, deep hole—and the wolf tracks went right into it. The boys and Tiff came to a stop, staring ahead. Inside each of the boys' heads drummed the question, "What if...what if... *what if...*!" Tiff began to growl, quivering from the cold—and fright.

"Just then one of the Jewish religious teachers said to him, 'Teacher, I will follow you no matter where you go!' But Jesus said, 'Foxes have dens and birds have nests, but I, the Messiah, have no home of my own—no place to lay my head'" (Matt. 8:19-20).

Discussion Questions:
1. What had the boys found? Why was Tiff growling?
2. If we want to live as Christians, can we always stay comfortably at home, in familiar surroundings? What have Christians "given up" in order to follow Jesus Christ?
3. Compare living where you do to living in a wilderness. For what can you be thankful where you are? What has God—from His bounty—provided you?

85

Day 3

Ghost Stories

The boys, Tiff, and Grandpa cautiously moved around the deadfall. With each step the boys took, they expected to see a snarling wolf rush from the tangle of tree trunks and branches and attack them. Only when they were well away from the place did they begin to breathe normally.

Farther upriver, they came to a dam made of sticks and mud. Behind the dam was a frozen lake. Joshua was the first to climb atop the dam, and almost at once something dove from the frozen reeds near his feet and swam beneath the ice. "Beaver," Grandpa said, climbing up behind Joshua to point toward the center of the lake. There, an ice-crusted mound of sticks and dirt poked above the surface of the lake. "And that's their house—called a lodge."

They walked on through the forest for several hours, sometimes with Grandpa leading and sometimes with him following. Not once did they see the sun or any sign of human work. At last, the boys were tired of walking through the snow. They also were hungry—and beginning to wonder where they were. "Are we lost?" David asked quietly.

Josh and Chris looked around, and Chris said, "If we went back to the river and followed it, we'd find the camp—I think."

"But the river's a long way over there," Josh said, uncertainly pointing behind and to their left.

"Well, actually," Grandpa said, smiling as he led them toward a hilltop, "the camp's down there." When the boys gathered around him in a thin clump of elm trees on the hilltop, they looked down, across a half-mile wide valley, and saw their camp near the bend in the river. With sighs of relief and whoops of joy, they ran, rolled, and tumbled down the hill and raced across the valley to build up their fire.

Sitting around their fire that night, they again heard a wolf howl and another wolf answer from a mile or so in another direction. The boys shivered, and Tiff suddenly scrambled into David's lap. Nervously, Chris and Joshua laughed, pointing to the trembling Tiff. But their laughter soon died. Then Chris said, "Hey, I know what. Let's tell ghost stories!"

"Okay," Joshua said, snuggling down inside his goose-down coat. "You start off."

Chris told a spooky story about a Boy Scout who had to go into a haunted house and spend the night. "And he had *gray hair* when he came out!" he ended. Joshua and David laughed slightly. "Your turn," Chris said, looking at Joshua.

Joshua told a story about a group of men who had to walk through a canyon where a giant lived. The giant kept grabbing the last man in the line—until there was only one man left. "And you're *him!*" Josh said suddenly, grabbing Chris. Chris jumped backward, scaring David so much that he had to clamp one hand over his mouth to keep from screaming.

"Your turn," Josh laughed, looking at David.

Eyes wide, firelight flickering over his face, David slowly shook his head. "Uh-uh, not me," he said. "Tiff and I want to go to bed!" He stood, holding Tiff tightly against his chest, and went into the tent.

The night grew colder and colder, and the fire slowly died. Chris, Joshua, and Grandpa sat staring into the embers, watching the flickering orange and red glow. Softly, almost in a whisper, Chris asked, "Grandpa Wiggins, are there *really* ghosts—and things like that?"

Grandpa stirred the embers so that they burned more brightly; a cloud of sparks rose, swirling into the black sky. "Satan wants you to be afraid of lots of things—ghosts, witches, demons, even nighttime itself. If he can make you afraid enough, maybe you'll run away from God."

Chris looked at Joshua as though he had something he wanted to ask but was afraid to. Joshua nudged him and nodded toward Grandpa. Chris brushed snowflakes off his lap and quietly asked, "Can—is it possible for—well, I mean I saw this movie on television where a bunch of demons took over this little girl's body and made her do awful things. Could *we*—could *I* get taken over like that?"

"Not if you stay *in* Jesus Christ," Grandpa said, looking seriously at both boys. "Paul, in Romans 8:38-39, said, 'For I am convinced that nothing can ever separate us from his love. Death can't, and life can't. The angels won't, and all the powers of hell itself cannot keep God's love away. Our fears for today, our worries about tomorrow, or where we are—high above the sky, or in the deepest ocean—nothing will ever be able to separate us from the love of God demonstrated by our Lord Jesus Christ when he died for us.' "

Discussion Questions:

1. Why didn't David want to tell a ghost story? Do you wish he'd stayed up long enough to hear Grandpa's answer to Chris's question?

2. How could fear (about the future, for example) make some people run away from God and toward things like witchcraft, astrology, and even things like guns, karate, and other methods of self-defense?

3. After reading the passage of scripture Grandpa quoted, *why* can't any of the things Paul listed separate us from the love of God? How, then, *should* Josh, Chris, and David feel about things like the wolf, ghosts, and the dark woods?

Day 4

The Whole Armor

During the night, the boys heard the wolves howl several times, and once it seemed as though they were very near the camp. The boys scrambled close to Grandpa, and Tiff—inside David's bedroll—whined. In the morning, the boys found several sets of tracks around the camp where more than one wolf had sniffed here and there.

Looking at the tracks, Chris whispered to Joshua, "They're *huge!* At least four inches across!"

"The snow melts around tracks," Grandpa explained as he came to the boys, "and makes them *look* bigger."

Nevertheless, the boys were very impressed, and they found themselves reluctant to leave the campsite—even when Grandpa pointed to a herd of deer that was watching the boys from the edge of the forest. "Do you want to follow the deer?" Grandpa asked. "Maybe we can see a porcupine or some other animals."

Joshua and Chris looked toward the dark trunks of the snow-laden trees and the shadows among them. "No thanks," Josh said.

"I can see," Grandpa said seriously, "that it's time you boys had something to think and dream about besides wolves and shadows and ghosts. Come inside the tent."

They followed him into the tent out of the cold wind and watched him get his Bible from his pack. As he opened it, he said, "I'm going to dress you boys."

"You're going to do what?" David asked, laughing as he glanced at Josh and Chris—then down at his thickly clad body.

Grandpa gave all three of them a look such as a general might give his soldiers before a battle. "In this world, you three are warriors. The battles you fight are against fear, temptations, and people who try to hurt you or make you do bad things. If you were warriors back in the time when everybody lived close to wolves, you'd have to get a gun or a sword to protect yourselves. But you aren't ordinary warriors; you're warriors for the King of Light—Jesus Christ.

"*His* warriors are given special equipment, and I want to read you Ephesians 6:10-17. As I read about each piece of 'equipment,' I want you to close your eyes and imagine that Jesus is putting it on your body. When you open your eyes, the armor will be there, but nobody will be able to see it—except you. Even though it's invisible, however, you can use it just like warriors of old used their armor—though yours will be a lot stronger." He began to read:

"Last of all, I want to remind you that your strength must come from the Lord's mighty power within you. Put on all of God's armor so that you will be able to stand safe against all strategies and tricks of Satan. For we are not fighting against people made of flesh and blood, but against persons without bodies—the evil rulers of the unseen world. . . . So use every piece of God's armor to resist the enemy whenever he attacks, and when it is all over, you will still be standing up. But to do this, you will need the strong BELT of truth and the BREASTPLATE of God's approval. Wear SHOES that are able to speed you on as you preach the Good News of peace with God. In every battle you will need faith as your SHIELD to stop the fiery arrows aimed at you by Satan. And you will need the HELMET of salvation and the SWORD of the Spirit—which is the Word of God."

When the boys opened their eyes, they were smiling. They looked at each other as though looking for the armor, then grinned at Grandpa. He closed the Bible and said, "Now, when you go to sleep tonight, instead of imagining things like wolves and ghosts, think about your armor—how it looks, how it feels, and most of all what you can do with it!"

Discussion Questions:
1. What were the two different kinds of armor Grandpa mentioned? Which kind is for "worldly warriors" and which kind is for Christians? Which kind will grow stronger the more it is used?
2. How is the Word—the Bible—like a sword? (See Hebrews 4:12.)
3. What do you suppose Chris, Joshua, and David will have to do before they can really feel like—or believe—that they are wearing the "whole armor of God"?

Day 5

The Wolf

Very early the next morning, Tiff began barking furiously. But quite suddenly he stopped and whined softly a few times. All three boys scrambled out of their sleeping bags and stuck their heads out the flaps of the tent. They glanced around and stopped—speechless.

Halfway between their camp and the dark forest stood a timber wolf. It was a male, and he was standing broadside to the boys—watching them. They saw his great, black and gray form clearly; he stood almost three feet tall at the shoulders and was nearly twice as long, not counting his bushy tail. His orange eyes were slanted, his muzzle sharp, and his breath came gusting out as white frost—as though he had been running. In his open mouth, the boys saw long, curved teeth. Their eyes grew wide as the wolf clicked his jaws together once.

Slowly, the boys' fear of the beast lessened, then faded. They recognized that he was not simply a terrifying animal who could easily tear them to pieces, but a majestic lord of the forest. He seemed unafraid, curious, wondering about the staring humans who had invaded his domain. Then, quite suddenly, he picked up a dead rabbit he had dropped in the snow and trotted into the forest in the direction of the den. In moments, he had faded from sight into the deep shadows of the forest.

"Did you see that?" Joshua whispered, grabbing Chris.

"Y-e-a-h," Chris breathed, looking down at David, who was lying flat on the floor of the tent, spellbound.

"Boy, wait'll Monday when we go back to school!" Joshua said, putting on his coat to go outside. "They won't *believe* what we saw!"

"Aw, they'll just say, 'So what?' " Chris muttered, zipping his coat to join Joshua. "We'd better just let it—him—be our secret."

Thoughtfully, Joshua nodded, grinning as he stared in the direction the wolf had gone.

After they had packed and carried everything back to Grandpa Wiggins' car, the boys were about to get in when they stopped. They stared at the forest, then looked at Grandpa with huge smiles.

"Thanks, Grandpa," Joshua said, going to hug the old man. "This's been the best adventure *ever!*" '

"Yeah, thanks, Mr. Wiggins," Chris and David echoed, also going to Grandpa.

He put his arms around their shoulders, and they gave the forest one final look. Quietly—so quietly that he did not disturb the silence of the snowbound wilderness—Grandpa said, "There's one adventure that may be better—much better—than this one; it's an adventure you can spend the rest of your lives doing—*if* you keep your armor on!"

"For the Holy Spirit, God's gift, does not want you to be afraid of people, but to be wise and strong, and to love them and enjoy being with them. If you will stir up this inner power, you will never be afraid to tell others about our Lord. . . . You will be ready to suffer with me for the Lord, for he will give you strength in suffering" (2 Tim. 1:7-8).

Discussion Questions:
1. In what two different ways did the boys see (or think of) the wolf? What made the difference between the two ways?
2. What adventure was Grandpa Wiggins talking about that might be *better* than the boys' adventure in the wilderness? How would the above scripture passage help them in that adventure?
3. What benefits can we gain from suffering (or hardship)? Why is it a good idea to be prepared—and to know from where and how we can get help—for times of suffering?

You Will Know Them by Their Fruits

Day 1

Spring Cleaning

The school year crept by and the weather gradually warmed as spring approached. With the warmer weather, the boys—Joshua, Chris, and David Matthews—remembered the clubhouse in the bois d'arc tree. They began to talk about getting it in shape for the summer—the first summer they would not have to look forward to going back to elementary school.

"Just think," Joshua said as they tramped across the rain-soaked fields toward the clubhouse, "next year we'll be in junior high."

"I wonder what it'll be like?" Chris muttered, looking down at the thick mud clotting on his shoes—and wondering if he could scrape it off before his mother caught him.

"My sister Janice says it's fun," Joshua replied, "but she also says some of the boys are pretty tough."

"We can handle 'em," Chris said confidently, grinning at David. It was then that Chris and Josh remembered that David was a year behind and wouldn't be going to junior high next year. He looked sad.

"It's okay," Joshua assured him, seeing his expression. "We'll still play with you, and you can still join the club—the King's Kids—just like we said."

"Are you still gonna let the *girls* join?" David asked, wiping his nose.

"Sure," Josh answered, glancing at Chris. He and Chris had decided that their club should grow—at least to include Lori Matthews and Janie Warren. And that also meant letting in Denise Kibler and, of course, David. "But that's okay," Josh said. "We're all friends."

"Look," Chris whispered, running ahead to the tree where the clubhouse stood twelve or so feet above the ground. He knelt at the base of the tree and touched several footprints with his fingertips. "Somebody's found our secret place."

Josh looked up at the two-story clubhouse of old boards they had built on the platform. "I don't think they hurt it," he said, starting to climb up. He went cautiously, watching out for an ambush.

When he reached the platform, he went into the lower room of the clubhouse, followed by Chris and David. "What're those?" Josh asked, pointing to a pile of colorful magazines thrown into one corner.

"Oh, boy!" David said, practically diving for the top magazine. "My mother won't even let my dad look at those kinds of magazines!" He hurriedly opened the magazine, looking wide-eyed at the pictures of the women inside. "I've always wondered. . . Wow!"

Chris looked at Joshua, who said, "I wonder who brought them up here?"

Chris shrugged with a funny expression. "I don't know, but I feel like our clubhouse has been—messed up."

Joshua looked at Chris. "You know what we oughtta do, don't you?"

"Yeah," Chris said slowly, looking at David and the open magazine, "but do you want to look at them first?"

Joshua squirmed, frowning. "Naw," he finally said. "Think I'll climb up and see if they did anything to the top room." He went to the ladder and climbed up until he could open the trapdoor. Then he went on up into the top room, leaving Chris to look down at the magazine David was turning through. Josh called down, "There's a wine bottle up here with a little bit of wine in it." He climbed down the ladder—and saw Chris standing by David, holding the stacked magazines in his arms. David had a sour look, but he didn't say anything.

"What do you think we should do with the stuff?" Chris asked, looking at the wine bottle Joshua was carrying.

"Is that old shovel still under the leaf pile with the boards?"

"I guess so—if our raiders haven't stolen it."

Joshua nodded and began climbing down the tree. Halfway down, he stopped, looked up at Chris—who was watching him—and smiled. "Black Bart strikes again!" he said, then dropped to the ground.

" 'The laws of Moses said, "You shall not commit adultery." But I say: Anyone who even looks at a woman with lust in his eye has already committed adultery with her in his heart' " (Matt. 5:27-28).

"And remember, when someone wants to do wrong it is never God who is tempting him, for God never wants to do wrong and never tempts anyone else to do it. Temptation is the pull of man's own evil thoughts and wishes. These evil thoughts lead to evil actions and afterwards to the death penalty from God" (James 1:13-15).

Discussion Questions:
1. In this chapter, by what were the boys tempted? How—and why—does someone become evil? What is "evil"? (See John 3:19-20.)
2. Even if a person did not *do* anything wrong, how might that person still be evil? Why is the penalty for evil, death? (See 1 John 1:5.)

Day 2

Return of the Raiders

The members of the King's Kids club were painting the clubhouse one Saturday in May when they heard voices coming through the woods. Josh looked out. "I think our raiders are coming back."

Chris and he climbed down; David, Lori, Janie, and Denise followed. Denise came to stand by Chris and Josh; her fists doubled up when she saw who was coming. "It's Richard, Sammy, and the other Scorpions," she said in a low voice. "I thought we'd be rid of them for the summer."

"They're back," Josh said. He raised his right hand, waved and called to Richard, " 'Lo. How're you doing?"

Richard, wearing a dirty white jacket lettered "Scorpions!", came to within ten feet of the tree where the clubhouse was. He looked over each of the King's Kids with a sneer, then jerked his chin toward the clubhouse. "Thanks for paintin' up our place—but we want our magazines an' booze back. Soon as you give 'em back, you can leave, an' we won't hurt you." He laughed and turned to look at his four companions.

"Richard," Denise snarled, "I'll break your face if you—!"

"It's okay," Josh said calmly. "Let's call it quits for today." He turned to gather up some tools.

"Not so fast," Richard replied. "We want our stuff!"

Josh looked at him. "We buried your magazines a long time ago, so they're probably rotted. And we dumped out your wine."

Richard's expression became angry, and he stepped toward Joshua. "Well, you can pay for them, then!"

"No way!" Chris said, getting set for a fight.

Calmly Joshua said, "We can't pay you for them. It wouldn't be a right way to spend God's money."

"God's money!" Richard whooped. He turned to grin at his friends, then sneered at Joshua, "What are you, some kind of religious nut?"

"Yes," Josh said, "a Christian. And this clubhouse isn't ours to give you anymore than our money is ours to give you. The clubhouse and our money belong to God. We gave it to Him."

"You what?" Richard demanded; he looked astounded. When Joshua didn't repeat himself, Richard glanced up at the clubhouse with a frown. "Just show us where you buried the magazines an' we'll leave you alone," he finally said.

"They're buried in the creekbank," Chris said, pointing toward a tree.

"What'd you do that for?" Richard practically whined. "There wasn't anything *wrong* with them. We lifted 'em from a drugstore."

"We just didn't want them around where God is," Joshua replied.

Again, Richard stared at him as he might have stared at a Martian. "You didn't *what?*" he asked quietly, almost respectfully. He glanced up at the clubhouse again, then at the members of the King's Kids. When they didn't say anything, he said, "Say, listen; my parents are religious, too, but my dad reads magazines like those. And where do you think the wine came from? Huh? Grapes that *God* made, right?"

Joshua didn't answer; none of the other King's Kids did either.

Richard, in a defensive tone, said, "Look, things like that were put here to enjoy. What's wrong with a little enjoyment?" he asked loudly. "That doesn't make somebody a murderer or anything, does it? I mean, stuff like wine or sexy pictures or—or even marijuana is just for *fun*. Don't tell me you're against *fun!*" He looked demandingly at Josh and the other King's Kids, but none of them said a word.

Abruptly, Richard laughed and spread his hands apart. "Aw, come on. You gotta be *free*. God *lets* us have stuff like that, so we must be free to use them an' have fun with them—right?"

"These men are as useless as dried-up springs of water, promising much and delivering nothing; they are as unstable as clouds driven by the storm winds. They are doomed to the eternal pits of darkness. They proudly boast about their sins and conquests, and, using lust as their bait, they lure back into sin those who have just escaped from such wicked living.

" 'You aren't saved by being good,' they say, 'so you might as well be bad. Do what you like, be free.'

"But these very teachers who offer this 'freedom' from law are themselves slaves to sin and destruction. For a man is a slave to whatever controls him" (2 Peter 2:17-19).

Discussion Questions:
1. How did Joshua deal with Richard and the other Scorpions? What do you think made it possible for him to treat them the way he did?
2. Why do you suppose Richard was so surprised by Joshua's answers? Why do you suppose Richard stopped demanding the clubhouse and money?
3. Why did the other King's Kids go along with Joshua and not say anything? To whom is Josh a slave? To what is Richard a slave? Is anybody *not* a slave of someone or something?

Day 3

Night Attack

"Look what they did!" Chris stormed, kicking one of the broken boards that had fallen from the destroyed clubhouse. "They must've come back last night with—with crowbars or axes."

Joshua and David were busy picking up boards that were still usable. Josh paused and looked up at the wrecked clubhouse. "I feel sorry for them," he said quietly.

"I don't!" Chris muttered. "I think we ought to go find them and *make* them pay—make them fix it up!"

"Like they tried to make us pay for those magazines?" Josh asked, grinning at his friend.

"Well, this is different," Chris muttered. "What we did was right, and what they did was wrong."

"Do you think *they* thought it was wrong?" Josh asked, laying several boards on a pile he and David were making.

Chris looked up at the platform—which was still intact—and finally said, "No, probably not. They probably figured we had it coming, that they had a right to get even with us."

"Do you remember that weird woman who was hanging around outside school last month?" Josh asked, sitting down to rest.

"Yeah," Chris said, frowning as he came to sit by Joshua. David went on picking up pieces of the clubhouse. "The one who was trying to give kids pamphlets about her religion—and bumming change from the teachers," Chris added, grinning slightly as he shook his head. "Yeah, she was weird all right—even though if you just looked at her, she seemed to be okay."

"Well, she thought *she* was right, too," Joshua said. "In fact, she said that everything she was doing was 'in the name of God.'"

"Yeah," Chris said slowly, remembering. Then he frowned. "But in the Bible it says, 'He who does not work shall not eat.'* And she

---

*2 Thessalonians 3:10

101

wasn't working; she was bumming."

"So," Joshua said thoughtfully, "what Grandpa told me one time seems to fit both that woman and the Scorpions: If somebody persists in doing what's wrong, God lets them think they're right. If God *made* everybody think *His* way, then we wouldn't be free anymore and we wouldn't be human anymore either. Grandpa says that being human means we have the freedom to choose and the thinking ability to choose and the will to do what we choose to do—right or wrong."

Chris thought about it; finally he sighed. "Let's get back to work," he suggested, frowning as he looked at the mess.

"[This man of sin] will completely fool those who are on their way to hell because they have said 'no' to the Truth; they have refused to believe it and love it, and let it save them, so God will allow them to believe lies with all their hearts, and all of them will be justly judged for believing falsehood, refusing the Truth, and enjoying their sins" (2 Thess. 2:10-12).

Discussion Questions:
1. How did Chris feel toward the people who wrecked the club-house? How did Joshua feel toward them? Why do you suppose Joshua felt the way he did? Do you think he forgave them in his heart?
2. How can many people do what they claim is right—and even do things in the name of God—but still be wrong, even evil? (See 2 Peter 2, especially verses 1-3.)

Day 4

Day Attack

Joshua, Chris, and David were working on rebuilding the club-house the Saturday before school was out when they saw Richard coming through the woods. With him was another of the Scorpions, Sammy Fletcher. Both boys had their hands stuffed in the pockets of their jackets; they looked casual and not at all like enemies. In fact, as they climbed up to the platform, they brought some boards with them from the pile.

" 'Lo," Joshua said, laying down his hammer and sticking out his right hand to shake with Richard. "Glad to see you."

Richard stared at him for several moments, laid down the boards he had brought up, and hesitantly shook hands with Josh. He nodded to Chris and David. "How're you doin'?" he asked, looking around. "Say, what happened here? Looks like a disaster."

Joshua shrugged, looking at the partially rebuilt walls. "Some-body tore it up, but we're going to build it back better than before. It's going to be *four* stories high this time." He grinned at Richard and added, "By the way, you're welcome to join the King's Kids if you want to." He looked at Sammy Fletcher. "You can too."

"Naw," Richard said, sitting against one wall. "We got our own club." Slowly, he began to grin. "But I gotta admit, you guys have a pretty good idea—gettin' girls to join your club. Bet you have lots of fun up here with them where nobody can see you."

Josh quickly stuck out one arm to stop Chris from knocking Rich-ard in the head with a hammer. He pushed Chris back and sat down facing Richard, glancing up at Sammy, who was standing in the door-way. "Well, I'll tell you how it is with having girls up here," Joshua said slowly, looking Richard in the eyes. "God's Word—the Bible—says, 'Sexual sin is never right: our bodies were not made for that, but for the Lord, and the Lord wants to fill our bodies with himself!'* So, that's just what we do."

---

*1 Corinthians 6:13

103

Richard snorted uncomfortably, glancing at Sammy. "That's what you *don't* do, you mean. Boy, you guys are dumber than I thought!" Joshua started to say something, but Richard quickly raised both hands. "No, don't quote any more Bible stuff at me," he said with a mock pleading look. "I get enough of that from my mother!" He laughed, looking at Sammy Fletcher, and pushed his companion out the doorway. "Come on, Sammy; let's get outta here before this religious stuff rubs off on us!" He laughed again, then followed Sammy down the steps on the trunk of the tree.

Joshua called after them, "Don't forget, you guys can join the King's Kids, too."

"Naw," Richard called back. "That'd mean giving up the Scorpions, and we *couldn't do that!*" Laughing, shoving Sammy ahead of him, he soon disappeared into the forest.

"Haven't you yet learned that your body is the home of the Holy Spirit God gave you, and that he lives within you? Your own body does not belong to you. For God has bought you with a great price. So use every part of your body to give glory back to God, because he owns it" (1 Cor. 6:19-20).

Discussion Questions:
1. How did Chris react (what did he start to do) when Richard suggested that the boys might be doing bad things with the girls in the clubhouse? How did Joshua react?
2. Why does Joshua keep offering to let Richard and the other Scorpions join the King's Kids?
3. How do you think Sammy Fletcher feels about the way Richard treats him?

Day 5

New Members

The King's Kids were having their first club meeting of the summer. They were *happy*—school was out, three months of vacation lay waiting ahead of them, and Sammy Fletcher had decided to join their club. He was sitting at one side of the four-story clubhouse's bottom room, listening to the other kids making plans for a party at Denise's house.

"My father volunteered to help hang balloons and crepe paper," Denise said, "and my mother said she'd bake cookies for all of us."

"I've got some records I can bring," Chris said, "and a record player."

"Okay," Joshua said, checking items off a list on a piece of paper he was holding. "If Janie and Lori can bring sandwiches and chips and stuff, and David will bring those games he was talking about, that just leaves getting something to drink. I guess I could—"

Sammy Fletcher cleared his throat and scooted hesitantly into the circle. "I could—I mean, what do you guys want to drink?"

"How 'bout a few quart bottles of soda pop?" Josh asked.

When the group members nodded, Sammy said, "Okay, I'll bring the drinks."

In their busyness they hadn't heard footsteps cautiously climbing the steps on the tree trunk. They were surprised when someone said, "Can I bring something, too?"

They all turned—and saw Richard standing in the doorway, looking uneasily at them. Joshua stood quickly and went to him, grinning. "Come on in," he said cheerfully.

"You're not mad at me?"

"No," Joshua said, blinking. "I'm *glad* to see you. Want to come to our party?"

"Sure—if you want me." He then saw Sammy Fletcher sitting with the group—and looking like he'd been caught doing something wrong. "What're *you* doing here?" Richard asked Sammy.

"Same thing you are, I guess," Sammy said, grinning at the other kids. "I got tired of the Scorpions."

"Yeah," Richard muttered, scuffing one shoe on the floor of the clubhouse and staring down. "Me too." He looked at Joshua with an odd expression. "Thanks," he said quietly.

"What for?" Josh asked.

"For—for not being mad at me—for what we—I did."

"Like I said, I'm just glad you're here."

"All right!" Richard said more loudly, rubbing his hands together. "When's the party, and what can I bring?"

"So, warmly welcome each other into the church, just as Christ has warmly welcomed you; then God will be glorified" (Rom. 15:7).

Discussion Questions:
1. What decisions did Sammy and Richard make? Why do you suppose they decided to join the King's Kids?
2. Is Christianity some kind of club that only certain people—people who are "good enough" or have money or status—can join? (See Matthew 9:10-13.) How might Richard's and Sammy's lives have been different if Joshua and the other King's kids had taken an "eye for an eye" attitude toward them?
3. What is the "proof" that someone is a Christian—a follower of Christ? (See Matthew 7:17-27, especially verse 20.)

Mrs. Wards' Dog

Day 1

Trouble!

The instant Joshua opened the front door of his house, David Matthews rushed in—carrying his dog, Tiff, in his arms. "We've got trouble!" he said breathlessly.

"You mean, about the dogs that have been poisoned?" Josh asked, leading David into his room.

"Yeah," David said, holding Tiff tighter. "You've heard?"

"Dad and Mother were talking last night," Josh said, "and they said old Mrs. Wards' dog was the third dog around here poisoned this summer. The first one was—"

"I know, I know!" David interrupted. He frowned, looking down at Tiff—who obviously would rather have been running around, sniffing the room. "But we gotta catch the murderer before—before..."
He looked at Joshua as tears brimmed his lower eyelids.

Joshua went to his bed and sat down. "It could be anybody."

"Not anybody!" David declared. "Old Mr. Clardy is doing it! He hates dogs—and kids—cutting across his yard. He gets *furious* every time he catches a kid or a dog or even a *cat* in his yard."

"Yeah, I know. But he lives quite a ways from here, and Mrs. Wards' dog was poisoned in her backyard. She really depended on the little thing; it was her only friend. It barked when the telephone or doorbell rang 'cause Mrs. Wards was too hard of hearing to hear them. And it used to—"

"But don't you see?" David persisted. "That means the murderer is *nuts*! I mean, nobody but *nobody*—except a nut—hates dogs so much that they'd throw poisoned meat into an old lady's yard to kill her dog!" Close to tears, he hugged Tiff against his chest again. Tiff grunted and squirmed to get down.

"I agree," Joshua said patiently. "Only a nut would do such a thing. And that rules out Mr. Clardy. He thinks a whole lot of his yard—and not a whole lot about kids and dogs—but he isn't a nut. Besides, I'm more worried about Mrs. Wards. What's she going to do now—for a friend and for someone to bark at her when she leaves something cooking on the stove and it starts to burn? We ought to. . ."

David, clutching Tiff, left the room, saying, "I'll see you later. I gotta get the club members together. Maybe we can keep watch at night and catch the murderer before he gets anybody else's dog!" Without waiting for Joshua to say anything else, David left, slamming the door.

" 'Then I, the King, shall say to those at my right, "Come, blessed of my Father, into the Kingdom prepared for you from the founding of the world. For I was hungry and you fed me; I was thirsty and you gave me water; I was a stranger and you invited me into your homes; naked and you clothed me; sick and in prison, and you visited me."

" 'Then these righteous ones will reply, "Sir, when did we ever see you hungry and feed you? Or thirsty and give you anything to drink? Or a stranger, and help you? Or naked, and clothe you? When did we ever see you sick or in prison, and visit you?"

" 'And I, the King, will tell them, "When you did it to these my brothers you were doing it to me!" ' " (Matt. 25:34-40).

Discussion Questions:
1. What was the main thing about which David was concerned? How was David's concern right—and wrong? With what was Joshua more concerned?
2. With what was Jesus Christ most often concerned? About what did He become angry? What, then, is the main duty for Christians?

Day 2

The Guards

The King's Kids met at David and Lori Matthews' house after supper that night. They all had heard about the poisonings, and they all were upset because all of them except Joshua and Chris owned a pet dog.

"I say we should spread out and keep watch near every house where there's a dog," David insisted.

"Sure, I can see us standing around alleys and in the bushes," Lori said, giving her brother a look as though he were a turnip. "The grown-ups ought to be really thrilled about that."

"Well, they know what's going on. They won't mind if they know we're trying to catch the murderer," David argued.

"But we might have to stand out there all night," Chris protested, trying to think of a better way to do things.

"So?" David asked. "I never knew you to want to go to bed early." The others laughed, and Chris grinned.

"It would be a good excuse to get to stay out late," Chris agreed.

While the others were thinking, Joshua said, "Has anybody thought about what we can do for Mrs. Wards?"

They looked at him as though he suddenly had started speaking Chinese. "Like what?" Janie asked. "Her dog's dead. We can't—"

"I guess we could get her another dog," Denise suggested.

"My uncle lives on a farm and raises fox terriers!" Richard said, leaning forward. "He'd probably give me a puppy if he knew what it was for."

"That's a good idea!" several of the kids exclaimed.

"But what I was thinking about was *right now*," Joshua said. "My folks said Mrs. Wards *depended* on her dog."

"Well, I guess we could give her the money we've been saving up," Lori suggested. "Maybe she could hire somebody to come in for a day or two—until Richard could get a puppy from his uncle."

111

"Hey!" David said, standing. "What about the other dogs in the neighborhood? Helping Mrs. Wards get another dog is fine, but what about keeping the other dogs *alive?*"

So it was decided: Guards would be posted at the end of each alley. In that way, the club could cover four blocks. The members fanned out, first to tell the people in the houses nearest where they'd be hiding what they'd be doing, and second to hide in the shadows.

An hour, then another . . . and another went by. Occasionally, one of the guards would whistle softly, and the others would answer to let one another know they were still in position. But other than a few people walking or jogging down the streets, they saw no one—least of all the murderer.

" *'Ask, and you will be given what you ask for. Seek, and you will find. Knock, and the door will be opened. For everyone who asks, receives. Anyone who seeks, finds. If only you will knock, the door will open'* " (Matt. 7:7-8).

Discussion Questions:
1. What does Joshua want to do that the others don't—or haven't really heard him say yet?
2. If Joshua were praying about the situation, for what do you think he would pray?
3. For what can we ask God? How can we know what we should ask for? Will He always answer in the way we expect Him to? To help you answer these questions, consider the fact that Jesus prayed, *"May [God's] will be done here on earth, just as it is in heaven"* (Matt. 6:10), and that the Apostle Paul wrote, *". . . try to find out and do whatever the Lord wants you to"* (Eph. 5:17).

Day 3

The Visit

The next day was Thursday—three days after Mrs. Wards' dog had been poisoned and a week since the poisoning before that. Joshua was up and out early, having decided to visit Mrs. Wards on his own. He was walking up the street, wondering whether he should tell her about what Richard planned to do when he heard a truck roaring up behind him. He turned quickly and had to jump up on the curb to keep from being hit by a garbage truck. The driver stopped it and jumped down, glaring at Joshua as he grabbed two sacks of garbage from the edge of a yard and threw them into the back of his truck. Then he drove on, giving Josh another glare. *Must've had a bad morning*, Josh thought, walking on toward Mrs. Wards' house.

When he finally knocked on her kitchen door loudly enough for her to hear, she opened the door only an inch or so. "Who is it?" she shouted.

"Joshua Wiggins," Josh called in return.

"Dan's grandson?" Mrs. Wards shouted.

"Yes, ma'am," Josh answered, a little embarrassed at having to shout.

She opened the door slowly and let him in. Pulling a housecoat tightly about her stooped body, she went to the kitchen table. "Sit down—sit down!" she said. "Would you like a glass of water?"

"No, ma'am. I just came by to see if you needed anything."

"I'm sorry, but I don't have any soft drinks—or cookies to offer you," Mrs. Wards said, frowning sadly as she peered at Joshua.

Josh realized he hadn't spoken loudly enough. "That's all right," he yelled. "I just wanted to see if you needed anything! Can I do anything for you?"

Mrs. Wards' face lighted up, and she raised one hand. "Oh, goodness! You don't want to be fooling around with an old lady's problems. Do you?"

"I've got all day," Josh shouted. "Just tell me what you need done!"

She did. First one thing, then another. Joshua soon realized that she was having him do mainly things that didn't really need being done; she was just keeping him around to have somebody to talk to and to be with. He grinned to himself and thought, *That's okay, too.*

"*'Anyone wanting to be a leader among you must be your servant. And if you want to be right at the top, you must serve like a slave. Your attitude must be like my own, for I, the Messiah, did not come to be served, but to serve, and to give my life as a ransom for many'*" (Matt. 20:26b-28).

Discussion Questions:
1. What were two things that happened to Joshua that might have made his day a bad one? How did he deal with those things?
2. Why didn't Joshua just *tell* the other King's Kids to come with him and visit Mrs. Wards?
3. In what sense did Jesus Christ "turn everything upside down"? (See the above scripture passage.)

Day 4

Presents

Janice let Richard into the house, and he went straight into Joshua's room. "I got it!" Richard whooped, holding up a white, black-spotted puppy. The puppy's tongue and tail were going ninety miles an hour, and Richard was having to hold his head back to keep from getting licked in the mouth.

"Hey, he's cute!" Joshua said, reaching to pet the puppy.

"Wanna take him to Mrs. Wards right now?"

"Does he have his shots?"

"Naw," Richard said, suddenly dejected. "My uncle said I could have the dog, but I'd have to pay for his shots."

Joshua snapped his fingers. "I know! We can use the club money we've been saving up—if everybody says it's okay."

So, they called a meeting. And, piled into the Wiggins' car, they all took the puppy to a veterinarian's office—and then to Mrs. Wards' home. Joshua—since he was used to talking to her—did the shouting for the whole group.

"Yes, ma'am, he's a *present!*" he told the old woman as the King's Kids stood around her in her kitchen. "We thought you'd need another dog!"

Tears spilled from her eyes and trickled down her cheeks as she held trembling hands toward the puppy. "He's—he's *just* like Pepper was when he was a puppy," she cried, taking the dog from Richard. Cuddling it against her, she whispered, "Thank you." She kissed Richard on one cheek, then Joshua and the others.

Richard squirmed with embarrassment and almost wiped off the kiss. But he didn't. Instead, he shouted, "We got him his shots, too! And my uncle said you'd be getting papers on him. He's *registered!*"

She held the puppy up. "Well, you're cute anyhow," she murmured, letting the puppy lick her nose and cheeks.

Richard, figuring she had misunderstood him, looked at Joshua, who simply grinned and shrugged.

Denise moved around in front of Mrs. Wards and spoke slowly so the old woman could see her lips. "Can we do anything for you while we're here? We'd be glad to clean the house for you—or maybe wash your dishes or—"

"Ma'am?" Janie said, coming to stand beside Mrs. Wards. "Can we just go to work? We promise we won't break anything, and we'll put everything back *just* the way you had it!"

Mrs. Wards held the puppy against her face, looking from one child to the next. She didn't seem a bit embarrassed at crying in front of them, but they became uncomfortable and wanted to get to work. "Thank you so much," she said, reaching toward them. "Thank you!"

" 'Take care! Don't do your good deeds publicly, to be admired, for then you will lose the reward from your Father in heaven. But when you do a kindness to someone, do it secretly. . . . And your Father who knows all secrets will reward you' " (Matt. 6:1, 3a, 4).

Discussion Questions:
1. Name some of the things the King's Kids did for Mrs. Wards. Which of these things do you think meant the most to her?
2. What do you think is the next temptation with which the kids are likely to be faced? (Note the above scripture.) What is the best way to deal with that kind of temptation?
3. Read 2 Corinthians 9:6-8. Why does God love a cheerful giver? In what ways were the King's Kids cheerful givers? In what ways are *you* a cheerful giver?

Day 5

The Murderer

Several of the King's Kids were walking up Joshua's street to Sammy Fletcher's house the following Monday morning. It was early in the day, and they all were going to a nearby park for a baseball game. Suddenly, Sammy came racing toward them. He slid to a stop and began stammering, "I saw him! I saw him!"

"Who? What're you talking about?" the others asked all at once.

"The murderer! Come on!"

They ran as fast as they could behind Sammy to his house. When they arrived, Sammy's mother was holding a chunk of meat away from their dog. Sammy's father was angrily talking to a garbage truck driver. Within minutes, a police car came speeding around the corner with its lights flashing. The car stopped in front of the Fletcher home, and everybody gathered around the garbage truck driver and Mr. Fletcher.

"But I didn't do nothin', I tell you!" the driver was yelling, waving his hands. He quieted down when he saw the policemen approaching.

"We were looking out the front window to make sure the dogs didn't tear up our garbage sacks," Mr. Fletcher said forcefully. "And we saw you drive up. When our dog ran out barking at you, you looked around to see if anybody was watching, then you took this piece of meat out of your truck and threw it to our dog. If my wife hadn't run out. . ."

"Yeah," the driver growled, rubbing his unshaven chin, "those blasted dogs! *You* let 'em run loose, barkin' at me, bitin' my legs, but when I try to do somethin' to protect myself, you call the cops!" He glared sullenly at Mr. Fletcher, then at the policemen. Finally, he glared at the kids. "What're *you* starin' at?" he demanded.

"Mrs. Wards' dog—a fox terrier—wasn't out chasing you," Chris stepped forward to state. "He was in his own backyard, minding his own business."

117

"That old lady's dog? The old lady who won't ever put her sacks out on the curb like she's supposed to?" the driver growled. "The one with the yappy little mutt who was always runnin' up to the fence, scarin' me when I was tryin' to do her a favor an' go pick up her garbage?"

"Yeah, some favor. Poisoning her dog," Chris said dejectedly.

"So what's the big deal?" the driver asked, turning to look at the policemen. "There ain't no law against killin' dogs. I didn't use no gun or nothin'. 'Sides, the animal control people wouldn't do nothin', an' my boss won't let us carry that spray can stuff like the postmen use." His look became even more sullen—and also pleading. He folded his arms and hunched his beefy shoulders. "I got sick of bein' bit, that's all." He looked at the ground and said nothing more.

One of the policemen came from the patrol car. To Mr. Fletcher, then to the driver he said, "If one of the neighbors who lost a dog wants to press charges, he can. Meanwhile, I've called this man's supervisor. They're sending another driver out. This one will be given disciplinary action."

"Aw, so what?" asked the driver. "I can always get another job!"

There were many things the kids wanted to say, but somehow there didn't seem much point in saying anything. The man obviously wasn't going to be made to feel guilty, and, in a way, the kids could sympathize with him. After all, several of the kids had been bitten by loose dogs while riding their bicycles, and they remembered the worry about getting rabies. So, they drifted away and set out toward the park again.

"At least they caught the murderer," David Matthews said, holding a baseball bat over one shoulder. "Now I can let Tiff out of my room."

The others grinned, feeling relieved. The mystery was solved; Mrs. Wards had been helped; and maybe a few people had learned lessons from the whole thing.

"Hey, you know," Sammy said, reaching down to pet his dog, who was following them, "it sure is a *beautiful* day!"

"Dear friends, never avenge yourselves. Leave that to God, for he has said that he will repay those who deserve it. Don't let evil get the upper hand but conquer evil by doing good" (Rom. 12:19a, 21).

Discussion Questions:
1. How might the whole problem of the poisoned dogs have been prevented? As Christians, what kinds of responsibilities do we

have to our neighbors and other people with whom we have contact?

2. Is it easy to leave justice in God's hands? What are some differences between human justice and God's justice?

3. Do you think the King's Kids will forget about Mrs. Wards now?

A Rose for Grandpa

Day 1

Please Don't Let Him Die

"Sure," Joshua whispered to Janice, "I knew he was eighty-six, but he hasn't been sick since he came to live with us after Grandma died."

"I just always thought he was *old*," Janice whispered back, "so I guess it doesn't surprise me."

"It's not that it surprises me," Josh said softly, glancing at the hospital room door across the hall, "it's just the *suddenness* of it. I didn't expect—"

"You can go in now," said a doctor, who had been standing in the door of the room where Grandpa Wiggins lay dying. Both children stood up, glanced at each other, and went hesitantly into the room.

Their mother and father were by the bed on which the old man lay. He was propped up slightly, and his hair was neatly brushed—it was almost as white as the pillow on which his head was lying. Equipment stood on the far side of the bed, flickering with lines of blue-green light. The equipment made small mechanical sounds as it monitored his heartbeat and breath rate.

Josh stood beside his grandfather's head as his mother moved over. He looked down at the pale, almost waxy-looking face he had loved all his life—a face that seemed to him to have always been the way it looked now. Only now the rosy tint was gone from the cheeks, and the sparkle was gone from the pale blue eyes. "Please, God," Joshua prayed silently, "please don't let him die."

Grandpa turned his head slightly, making the oxygen tube connected to his mask whisper across the sheets. He blinked and smiled faintly when he saw Josh. Janice was standing behind her brother, and she waved to her grandfather. "Hi, Grandpa," they both said quietly. He nodded, and his eyes drifted shut as though he were very sleepy.

"Hi, son," he barely said. His voice sounded strange through the plastic oxygen mask.

Josh felt a sudden urge to tear off the mask and the tubes going into his grandfather's body and run away with him. "I don't want you to die, Grandpa," he said, trying desperately not to cry.

Grandpa smiled faintly. "Sorry, son, but that's what I've spent my whole life getting to." After the effort to say that, he closed his eyes and breathed with difficulty for a while.

"You'll get better," Joshua said firmly, taking his grandfather's hand. He pushed up the plastic bracelet and patted the spotted, withered hand. "God won't let you die; I know He won't."

His grandfather opened his eyes and smiled faintly again—and this time a sparkle came into his eyes. "Josh, I hope He does. It's time, you know. I'm . . . just thankful . . . He let me live . . . this long." His eyes drifted shut, and fear surged through Joshua. He turned to his mother with a frightened look.

"He's asleep," his mother said. "Let's go now; we can come back later."

Josh looked tearfully at his grandfather and squeezed the relaxed hand tightly. There was no response; slowly Joshua let go. He glanced at the hand resting on the sheet, then followed his parents and sister from the room.

"For to me, living means opportunities for Christ, and dying—well, that's better yet" (Phil. 1:21).

Discussion Questions:
1. What do you think bothers Joshua most about his grandfather's dying? What does he pray—and expect—God will do? What would be the best thing he could pray for now?
2. Explain Paul's statement to the Philippians (quoted above). Do you ever fear death? Why or why not?

Day 2

It's Not Fair!

"It's not fair!" Joshua quietly told his mother in the hospital waiting room down the hall. "It's just not fair. He's a *good* man. He doesn't deserve to. . ." He couldn't say the word.

His mother looked patiently at him. "Josh, it's because he *is* a good man that he *does* deserve to die. People who aren't good—who aren't saved and who don't follow the Lord—are the ones who don't deserve to die. People like your grandfather will go to a place where the best part of them—their spirit—will be free to live forever in the full light of God's love. It's the other people—the unsaved ones—you should feel sorry for. When they pass through death, they'll know nothing but fear and darkness. And when they reach eternity, *all* the things they loved in this world will be gone; they'll have nothing but suffering."

"But the Bible says that the penalty for living a life of sin is death. Doesn't that mean that only bad people deserve to die?"

"What the Bible means is that the penalty for living a life of sin, living for yourself and the devil, is *eternal* death—eternal separation from God, His Light, and His love. The reason I said that unsaved people don't deserve to die is that I keep wanting them to have one more chance to listen, one more chance to repent and receive Christ into their lives. To me, it's sad—terribly sad—when someone dies who has refused to give his life to Jesus."

"What did Grandpa mean, 'It's time'?"

"He feels it's God's will that he go home now."

Joshua tightened up his mouth and hung his head. "God's will is hard sometimes, isn't it?"

His mother moved close to him and put one arm around his back so she could hug him against her. "If it seems hard, it's because you haven't understood how wise and loving God is. He *always* wants the best for His children, even if it means pain for them."

123

"Does God *make* people die?" Josh asked, looking up at his mother.

"If mankind never had sinned, there would be no death. But because the first people loved themselves so much that they wanted to become like God, death entered our world. When you're older, you'll see that death really is a blessing. Our bodies get old, unable to do things they once could do. We get sick; our friends die; day-to-day living becomes a painful, unhappy problem. How would you like to live forever in that way?"

"I'd rather be with Jesus," Joshua admitted. "But still..."

"Joshua," his mother said more firmly, straightening, "who are you thinking about more: yourself or Grandpa?"

He looked pleadingly at her. "But I'll miss him! I don't want him to die!"

"If you could, would you stop him from dying—if you knew it was God's will that he was supposed to die?"

Josh's face took on a troubled expression. "That would be a sin, wouldn't it—a bad one?"

His mother nodded seriously. "The desire to take things out of God's hands is where sin begins."

"You younger men, follow the leadership of those who are older. And all of you serve each other with humble spirits, for God gives special blessings to those who are humble, but sets himself against those who are proud. If you will humble yourselves under the mighty hand of God, in his good time he will lift you up. Let him have all your worries and cares, for he is always thinking about you and watching everything that concerns you" (1 Pet. 5:5-7).

Discussion Questions:

1. Describe Joshua's main problem in your own words. If you had that problem, how would you deal with it?
2. Suggest at least two reasons why people "take things out of God's hands." What are some things they take into their own hands? When someone does this, what usually happens? What can God do for that person or his/her problem?
3. What is the meaning of this statement: "Take all your problems to the foot of the cross, leave them there, and don't go back and pick them up!" If we go back and "pick them up," what does that show about how we trust God?

Day 3

In the Fields

Even though school had begun, and Josh was in junior high now—with homework to be done every day—he could think of only one thing: his grandfather. When the next Saturday came, and still the dreaded event had not taken place, Josh felt like he was about to explode. He took off alone, walking across the fields near his home.

At first, all he could see were the clods at his feet. Wheat had been harvested, the stubble plowed under, and the clods had been baked hard by the sun. As he stumbled over the rough ground, he kicked the clods and argued with himself.

"It's not fair!"

"You're not supposed to feel that way."

"But I *do*!"

"Stop it!"

He climbed through a fence and proceeded to walk across a pasture. Abruptly, he looked up and saw that he was almost face to face with one of the old bulls that lived in the pasture. Josh froze, wondering if he should try to run.

But the bull seemed in no mood for a chase—or anything but lazily chewing his cud, blinking flies away from his curly lashed eyes, and feeling the warm autumn sun on his back. So, Josh sat down, staring at the creature. "What do *you* think?" he asked it.

The bull's lower jaw worked side to side, around and around, and he continued to blink lazily.

"You don't think it's worth worrying about," Josh concluded, picking up a stone and hurling it across the pasture. He muttered, "I guess I'm just making myself sick with all this worrying. I *know* Grandpa will be better off in heaven, and I *know* how much he wants to be with Christ—but I don't know it, either. It's never seemed *real* 'til now." He looked at the bull again. "What do you think?" he asked it.

The bull's tail switched left and right against his broad back, sending flies whirling up—then back.

"Hmm, I guess you're right; I should be patient. Grandpa spent a *lot* of time trying to teach me that." He then went on remembering the things Grandpa had taught him—how to make a willow whistle, how to fish, how to read the Bible, to listen to and obey his parents.... There were just so many things. Joshua began to cry, looking at the bull. "I'm going to miss him," he whispered.

The bull suddenly stuck out his head and neck, opened his mouth, and bellowed! Josh scrambled to his feet and started to run, but then he turned and saw three cows coming across the pasture. He laughed nervously, wiping his tears. Looking back at the bull, he said, "Glad to see your friends, huh?"

That reminded him: Where had *his* friends been lately? He didn't remember seeing them much even at school. He walked on, kicking gopher mounds and thinking, *Even my friends are deserting me!* But quickly a thought popped into his head: *Whoa, wait a minute! Who's deserting who? You've been so concerned about your grandfather that you've practically forgotten your friends—and your father."*

Joshua stopped. "My father!" he said aloud. Suddenly, he began to realize what his father must be going through. His own father dying, nothing to be done, hospital bills mounting up, funeral preparations ... Joshua turned around and began running back across the pasture, scaring the cows so much they arched their tails over their backs and fled.

"When others are happy, be happy with them. If they are sad, share their sorrow" (Rom. 12:15).

"Share each other's troubles and problems, and so obey our Lord's command" (Gal. 6:2).

Discussion Questions:
1. What had Joshua "lost sight of" because of his concern for his grandfather?
2. If selfishness is a wall, what's on the other side? (From what does self-love separate us?)
3. What are some guidelines for helping others in times of trouble or sorrow? Don't people get tired of hearing "I'm sorry" over and over? If so, then what *does* help?

Day 4

The Last Rose

The hospital called late Wednesday night. Mr. Wiggins listened, finally said, "Yes—all right," and hung up. Turning to his watching family, he said, "Grandpa's dying."

While his mother got her coat, Josh went to do something he'd been thinking about. He found his pocket knife, ran outside to Grandpa's favorite rosebush, and cut the last bloom of summer. He trimmed the thorns from the stem and held the bloom to his nose, smelling the thick rich scent his grandfather had loved so much. Josh smiled at the rosebush, thankful it had bloomed one final time before the winter. He then ran back through the house and into the garage.

In the car, Joshua sat as close to his father as he could without getting in the way. When they got out at the hospital, Josh took his father's hand and held it as they walked into the building. He kept holding it until they gathered around Grandpa's bed.

"Can you hear me, Dad?" Mr. Wiggins said, bending close to his father's face. Grandpa weakly nodded. Mr. Wiggins said, "We love you!"

Josh held out the rose. His father smiled, lifted Grandpa's oxygen mask, and let Josh hold the dark red rose close. Briefly, Grandpa smiled. Slowly, his right hand came up, groping for the flower. Josh placed the stem in his hand and gently closed his fingers around it. He then helped Grandpa raise his hand until he could see the rose. Again, he smiled.

Then, slowly, his hand went down until it was lying on the sheets. Soon his fingers gradually uncurled from around the stem. Josh looked at Grandpa's face, and the words, "At peace, at peace," came into his mind. He heard his father crying, and he felt his father's arms around him as the family drew close together.

"And if being a Christian is of value to us only now in this life, we are the most miserable of creatures. But the fact is that Christ did

127

actually rise from the dead, and has become the first of millions who will come back to life again some day. Death came into the world because of what one man (Adam) did, and it is because of what this other man (Christ) has done that now there is the resurrection from the dead" (1 Cor. 15:19-21).

Discussion Questions:
1. What did Joshua do in this chapter to show his love?
2. How can we know that death is like a door or gate—not to be feared despite our natural feelings? (See Matthew 28:6.)

Day 5

Sorrow Into Joy

At the funeral Saturday, it didn't take Joshua long to figure out that something was wrong. His grandfather's casket was at the front of the church; he had stood with his family looking at Grandpa, and he had seen the same peaceful look on Grandpa's face that he had seen the night he had died. *That* was all right. But as Josh looked around at the two hundred or so people gathered in the church—aunts and uncles, cousins and nieces and nephews, friends of his parents and friends of Grandpa—he saw almost nothing but sad, downcast faces. That, to Joshua, seemed *wrong*.

Are they Christians or not? he wondered. *If they are, then why aren't they happy—joyful?* However, he remembered what his mother had told him as they were waiting to go from the funeral home to the church: "Stop grinning, Joshua; funerals are for the living, not the dead, and most of the living won't understand why you're smiling!"

"But they *should*," he had said. Her look had withered him.

And yet, it *was* wrong, he decided, looking around again. His mother gave him a sharp nudge, and he looked forward—toward the pastor, who was beginning to speak.

To Joshua's delight—and relief—the pastor seemed to have been reading his mind. As the text for his message, the pastor chose John 16:20, in which Jesus said to His disciples, "The world will greatly rejoice over what is going to happen to me, and you will weep. But your weeping shall suddenly be turned to wonderful joy [when you see me again]." The pastor went on to say, "And today, our brother—Daniel Mathis Wiggins—is filled with great joy, for he is beholding the face of our Lord." Joshua sighed; that was good enough for him!

His feeling of satisfaction continued as the funeral procession went to the cemetery. He stood with his family under a green tent by the grave and listened as the pastor and several men of the church told about Grandpa—what he had done, what kind of man he was, and what kind of Christian he was. Joshua looked around; although some people were crying, many others looked happy—as happy as he was. He realized, then, for the first time in his life, how *many* people had been touched by his grandfather's life. He saw people of all ages who had been in Grandpa's Sunday school classes. He saw people he never had seen before, all of whom—he felt certain—had been in some way helped by Grandpa. He saw Mrs. Wards and many of Grandpa's other friends, and he realized just how many friends Grandpa had had! Josh nodded slightly; his feeling of contentment and "rightness" was even stronger.

Before the casket was lowered into the grave, Josh and his family filed past it. Josh laid the rose he'd cut on top of the other flowers draping the casket; he murmured, "Good-bye, Grandpa—until . . ." With that, he felt that something had been completed—but not ended. As far as he was concerned, Grandpa was still alive—in things he had taught Josh, things he had done for him, and most of all in the way he had loved him. Josh went to his father, took one of his hands, and squeezed it.

"I heard a shout from the throne saying, 'Look, the home of God is now among men, and he will live with them and they will be his people; yes, God himself will be among them. He will wipe away all tears from their eyes, and there shall be no more death, nor sorrow, nor crying, nor pain. All of that has gone forever'" (Rev. 21:3-4).

Discussion Questions:
1. Talk about at least two things Joshua learned from his experiences at the time of Grandpa's death and funeral.
2. What is the greatest promise Jesus Christ made us? How do we claim that promise?
3. Imagine that you are to speak at the funeral of a person who died unsaved. What would you say?

Stand Fast!

Day 1

Changes

The remainder of that school year was difficult and confusing for Joshua—and for his friends. It seemed to Josh that he had been yanked out of childhood and dumped into a strange—and often hostile—world. Changes were happening to him so fast that he hardly had time to think about them, much less adjust to them.

The first change was the absence of Grandpa. Josh had been able to always go to Grandpa—for talk, for love, or just to have someone listen to him. Now that "someone" was gone. The next change was himself—he was becoming a man. He began staring into the mirror at his upper lip and watching his father shave. He was shy about his deepening—and sometimes cracking—voice, and he became more and more shy about his body. He was so shy that he didn't notice that the girls he knew were changing too; he only knew that he didn't like Lori anymore.

At about the same time, Chris stopped liking Janie Warren—or vice versa—and the King's Kids sort of broke up. Joshua was especially troubled about that change because in junior high school there were lots of gangs and groups, and without the King's Kids he felt alone. At one point, he even had a fight with Richard—who promptly went back into the Scorpions. Joshua felt terribly guilty about that, but he was so busy with his homework that he had little time to worry about anything very far beyond himself.

In the spring, he went out for track. He made the team, and he began to become part of a new group—one that often used language he had never heard, much less used; the guys told jokes about things he didn't understand—but was certainly expected to; and they discussed things he had never imagined. He also quickly learned that he was expected to be tough. He was challenged to two fights, both over things he hadn't noticed had offended anyone. He avoided the first fight, but the second one he could not avoid.

"Did you win?" his father asked, bending down to look at Josh's black eye and cut nose.

"Matt!" Mrs. Wiggins said, annoyed. "That's hardly the question to ask him." His father looked mildly ashamed and sat down to hide behind the evening newspaper. His mother took up the wet washcloth again and tried to wash more of the dried blood from the bridge of Josh's nose.

He squirmed. "Stop it! It hurts!"

She frowned at him. "Don't you talk back to me," she said quietly but very firmly. "You're not so big you can't still be spanked!"

Joshua slouched down into the couch, thinking, *I am too big to be spanked!*

Janice, who was sitting at the kitchen table doing homework, said, "Serves you right, Mr. Bigshot. You should've known better than to try to whip Frank Rothman."

"Shut up, Janice!" Joshua snapped, folding his arms.

"Don't talk to your sister that way," his mother said. "It isn't a bit nice."

"Well, did you hear what she said? I'm having enough trouble without her always butting in!" He stood angrily. "Nobody listens to me anymore! Everyone just puts me down and takes everybody's side but mine!" He stormed from the room.

"Don't copy the behavior and customs of this world, but be a new and different person with a fresh newness in all you do and think" (Rom. 12:2a).

Discussion Questions:
1. Name some of the pressures Joshua is facing that you've faced in your own life. Based on your experiences, what advice could you give Josh?
2. Why is it so hard not to "copy the behavior and customs of this world"? What kinds of pressures work on a Christian to make him or her forget about being a Christian? From whom do these pressures come?
3. What advice could you give Joshua's parents?

The Anchor

Joshua's school was farther from his home than his elementary school had been, so it took him longer to walk home. He used the time to think. One day, after track practice, he was very tired—so tired that he was almost dragging his feet. He flinched when a car honked its horn behind him. He turned with an angry look.

"Want a ride?" a man asked, leaning out the passenger side window. It was the pastor of Joshua's church.

Embarrassed at having looked so angry, Josh hurried to get into the pastor's car. "Sure," he said. "Thanks." He piled his books in his lap and sat staring ahead.

"You look as though you need a friend," Mr. Burton said pleasantly.

"Have you got one for me?" Josh asked. Only after he had said it did it occur to him that it sounded smart-alecky. He frowned, thinking, *What's happening to me? I've got to stop this.*

"Or maybe," the pastor continued, "you don't need a friend as much as you need an anchor."

"An anchor?" Joshua asked, looking for the first time at Mr. Burton.

"Sure. Boats adrift on the ocean sometimes need an anchor—before they drift in too close to the rocks and wreck themselves."

Josh somehow resented the comparison, and he looked ahead again. "I'm doing okay," he muttered.

"I'm sorry, but you don't look okay to me."

Josh shot him a close look. "Has my mother been talking to you?"

Mr. Burton looked surprised. "No, she hasn't. But I've seen a lot of pain in my career, so I know how to recognize it. You've got it."

Joshua bit his lip and slowly nodded.

"The anchor I'm talking about is an anchor that never moves—yet it can always be found. It never changes—even though different ships

135

on different seas use it. And it can be grabbed by anyone on board the ship—anyone who wants to, that is."

Joshua felt even more embarrassed than he had earlier. "You're talking about God, aren't you?" he asked. Mr. Burton said nothing.

When they stopped in front of the Wiggins' house, Joshua got out and turned around, holding the door open. "Thanks," he said. Hesitantly, he added, "I may come talk to you sometime—if you're not too busy to listen."

"I hope I can listen as well as your grandfather could," Mr. Burton said.

Joshua grinned, nodded, and carefully closed the door. He watched Mr. Burton drive off; he waved as the pastor turned the corner.

"For I am the Lord—I do not change. That is why you are not already utterly destroyed [for my mercy endures forever]" (Mal. 3:6).

Discussion Questions:
1. What did Mr. Burton offer Joshua besides a ride? Do you think it was by chance that he came by when he did?
2. Upon whom can we *always* depend—no matter what we've done or how we feel?
3. How did Mr. Burton treat Joshua? How *might* he have treated him? (What, for example, might he have said when Joshua turned around with an angry look?)

Day 3

Remembering

Although he had homework up to his ears, a track meet coming up, and was dog-tired, Joshua went to visit the pastor the next afternoon—after first calling the church to make sure Mr. Burton was free.

Joshua greeted him, laid his books on the floor of the pastor's study, and sank into an armchair.

"I'm glad you came," Mr. Burton began. "It took courage."

"Why?" Josh asked, surprised.

"As a guess, I'd say you're feeling guilty."

"Sort of," Joshua muttered, looking down at his hands.

"You're in junior high now, aren't you?"

"Yes, sir," Joshua said, sticking his hands between his knees.

"That probably means you're hearing even dirtier jokes than you heard in grade school, you're being pressured to prove how tough you are—more than in grade school, and you may even be feeling a little lost and alone in a school that's four times larger than your old one."

Josh began to grin. "You read minds pretty well," he said.

"And," Mr. Burton resumed, "I've heard you're on the track team. That probably means that you're having to learn how to compete *hard*, and how to 'psyche out' the competition. And you're probably pretty tired each night."

Joshua's grin broadened. "You remember, huh?"

"Yes," the pastor said, giving him a serious look. He sighed and leaned forward onto his desk. "Well, as you know, I'd rather tell stories than give advice, so—if you don't mind—I'll tell you a story. Then I'll listen. Okay?"

"Sure," Josh said, feeling more at ease now that he was sure the pastor wasn't going to criticize him.

Pastor Burton leaned back. "Once, there was a war going on—a big war. And there was a powerful King—a King more powerful than all the other kings put together. This King called all his subjects together. He gave each of them a gift—a wonderful, living gift. But because he wanted his subjects to keep their freedom and to keep on thinking and making decisions, he didn't force them to use their gifts in any one way.

"So, each of his subjects did with his or her gift what suited him or her. Some of the King's subjects placed their gifts on the mantel or high on a shelf—where they could be seen by everyone who came into their homes but where they wouldn't be in the way or get broken. Unfortunately, some of those homes were robbed, and the robbers took the King's gifts.

"Others of his subjects put their gifts in their front windows or on chains around their necks—again, so people could see and admire them. Unfortunately, the sun faded those people's gifts, and some were stolen. When others of the King's subjects heard about the thefts, they took their gifts and hid them away—in bank vaults, in mattresses and even in holes in the backyard. Unfortunately, when some of those people later checked on their gifts to make sure they were still as precious as when the King gave it to them, they found that the gifts had fallen apart and crumbled into dust.

"Still others of the King's subjects tried to make use of their gifts, figuring that the King wouldn't have given them something just for show or as wealth to be hoarded. Those people found some use for their gifts—as a crutch to help them through times of sickness, as a means of understanding some of the problems they'd been having, or as a way of feeling better about dying and the future. But, strangely, the King's subjects who only found a few uses for their gifts often were robbed. Renegades from the war outside the kingdom somehow got to those subjects who'd found only limited use for their gifts. And, still more strangely, those subjects readily gave up their gifts to the renegades, who quickly ran away. To the surprise of the renegades, the King's gifts soon turned into dust, and to the surprise of those who had easily let go of their gifts, they missed them more and more as time went by. In fact, they had to try many, many different things to forget the King's gifts.

"A few of the King's subjects, however, found that the more uses they tried to find for the King's gift to each of them, the more uses there were to find. These subjects used the gifts as tools, as weapons, as sources of comfort, for instruction, and on and on. They found that the more they used their gifts, the more valuable the gifts became—and the more useful they became.

"Eventually, these subjects discovered that their gifts could be used to fight the war that was going on all around them. The renegades fled from them when they used their gifts properly. The enemies of the kingdom were powerless against them. And the subjects who used their gifts properly were indestructible until God himself called them home. But, strangely, the others of the King's subjects never figured out how to use their gifts the way the few had done, even though there was no secret whatsoever about the gifts. Now what do you think of that?"

Joshua laughed easily. "I think it was a good story—and I think I'd better start remembering how to use the King's gift. I've sort of, uh, forgotten who I am."

"So, tell me about track. What events do you run?" Pastor Burton asked, leaning forward and smiling at Joshua.

"And let us not get tired of doing what is right, for after a while we will reap a harvest of blessing if we don't get discouraged and give up" (Gal. 6:9).

Discussion Questions:
1. What did Joshua mean when he said, "I've sort of forgotten who I am"? How might reading the above scripture verse help him?
2. What can Christians do when they get discouraged? (See Romans 12:5, 12-13.)
3. What do you think the King's gift in the story Pastor Burton told might be?

More Changes

"Mother, I'm sorry I've been talking back to you—and not acting very nice around here," Joshua said.

His mother laid down the shirt she'd been mending and came around the table to hug him. "I'm sorry, too, but I don't know if I can explain why. It's like—it's like I don't have my baby boy anymore and I don't quite know how to deal with the young man he's become."

He grinned.

"Frank, I'm sorry I got into that fight with you. I should have kept my temper better," Josh said, sticking out his right hand.

"You can cram your apologies in your left ear, Wiggins!"

"Lori, I'm sorry we stopped going steady, but couldn't we still be friends? I miss not having you to talk to—and to be my friend."

"Sure, we can be friends. Only, I'm going with Matt Winslow now, and he usually comes over in the afternoons to study, so don't call me then. Okay?"

"Richard, I'm sorry we had that dumb argument. I feel really guilty that I put you down. Forgive me?"

"Yeah, I forgive you," Richard replied, looking at his shoes. Then he looked into Joshua's eyes. "But it wasn't a 'dumb' argument. You were right—if that matters. I was going to tell you, but—well, I just didn't know how. And I also wanted to tell you I'm not in the Scorpions anymore—again." He grinned sheepishly. "Are the King's Kids still together?"

"No, but I'd like for them to be," Joshua said as they walked toward his locker.

"Say, Janice, do you suppose we could call a truce? I promise to stop calling you names, and I'm sorry for the times I've put you down."

She stared at him. "Are you for real?"

"You'll just have to watch me to make sure, won't you?"

"Well—okay."

"I love you, you know."

"Yeah, well, you're okay, too," she smiled, hugging him—for a second.

"So, my dear brothers, since future victory is sure, be strong and steady, always abounding in the Lord's work, for you know that nothing you do for the Lord is ever wasted as it would be if there were no resurrection" (1 Cor. 15:58).

Discussion Questions:
1. How did Joshua treat each of the people to whom he talked? How did he *not* treat them?
2. In what way(s) did "Black Bart" lose again?
3. What kind of "grade" would you give Joshua for courage? How might Philippians 4:13 have helped him?

Day 5

King's Kids Forever!

When the King's Kids finally got together again on a Wednesday night, school was almost out for the year. Jerry Cummins, the youth director of their church, sponsored the group—and provided the cookies and punch; but the group seemed to have about eight leaders, all of whom were talking at once. Finally, with a smile, Jerry gave up and let them talk.

"Look, we *need* each other," Richard was saying. "I get so that I think I'm the only one in school who's trying to be a Christian—unless I see one of you guys walking around looking the same way."

"Yeah, it helps to see each other, doesn't it?" Janie admitted. "If I get two sentences a day with Lori, I feel better. She just says, 'You hangin' in there?', and I go, 'Trying to,' or something. That helps—you know?"

"But we can't go around calling ourselves the King's Kids," Chris said. "People will think we're really weird or somethin'."

"What's wrong with saying—out loud, if necessary—that we're Christians?" Denise Kibler asked. "You ashamed of it?"

"No," Chris said defensively. "But I don't go around shoving it in people's faces, either. If they can't *see* what I am, then I'd be dumb to *tell* them."

"Unless they ask," Joshua said. "If somebody asks, 'Hey, what makes you so weird?', you gotta tell them." He grinned and several kids laughed.

"So, who else can we get to come Wednesday nights?" Sammy asked. "Not that I don't like you guys, but we need some more kids in here. We don't want to get reputations for being snooty, you know."

"People think we are anyhow," Lori said, "just 'cause we don't say 'Yes' when somebody offers us a joint or asks if we're going to the KISS concert or something."

"Who cares?" Richard said. "It used to bother me to be put down for not going out behind the bus garage to smoke. But now I just say, 'No.' If somebody pushes me, I tell 'em straight out, 'I don't do that.' They can take it or leave it."

"Shouldn't you tell them *why* you don't?" Janie asked.

Richard shrugged. "If they ask me when we're alone—so I know they're for real, I tell 'em."

"So who else . . . ?" Sammy repeated, more loudly than the first time.

"Well, there's Ebony DeGrate; she visited church last Sunday," Denise suggested. "And Toni Walters has been hanging around me like she wants to ask a question but is afraid to."

"How 'bout kids from the Sunday schools?" Joshua asked, turning toward the youth director. "Can you put up posters, Jerry?"

"No," Jerry grinned, "but you can."

"Hey, and there's Frank Rothman. Since he got cut from the football team, he's really been down," Chris suggested. "Maybe he could use a friend."

They went on naming people they planned to invite, and before long they began to grin at one another. They stopped talking when Joshua spoke up. "You know," he said, "before we're done, we'll have invited every kid in school. And you know what else? That's great, 'cause we need all the friends we can get!"

"[Jesus said,] 'Keep a sharp lookout! For you do not know when I will come, at evening, at midnight, early dawn or late daybreak. Don't let me find you sleeping. WATCH FOR MY RETURN! This is my message to you and to everyone else'" (Mark 13:35-37).

Discussion Questions:
1. In your own words, tell several of the things Jesus Christ expects us to do.
2. Describe some of the things that would tell you whether or not somebody is a Christian.
3. Tell how the following things were important to the King's Kids: the church, their parents, each other, Jesus Christ.